Reconciled by the Light

THE AFTER-DEATH LETTERS
FROM A TEEN SUICIDE

Reconciled by the Light

THE AFTER-DEATH LETTERS
FROM A TEEN SUICIDE

RON PAPPALARDO

ISBN 978-0-557-08969-7

To my wife, Connie,
and our children,
Joshua, Gabriel, Nadia, and Ari

ACKNOWLEDGMENTS

Although there have been innumerable people who have helped to make this book a reality, I would like to specifically thank the following:

Lynette Marks, for looking me in the eye and letting me know I <u>had</u> to tell this story.

The Rev. David and Takeko Hose for loving me and my family with a big heart.

Dr. Michael Peck and the doctors, nurses, and chaplains of the North Carolina Jaycee Burn Center at the University of North Carolina Hospital.

Michael and Kimberly Schlink for exemplifying true friendship.

Gayle Davis for exemplifying true Christ-like love and service.

Donnie Collier for being like a big brother.

Sam Uhl, for countless hours spent editing the manuscript.

Officer Bobby Beaman of the Cary Police Dept. for service above and beyond the call of duty.

Col. Thomas Finnerty for his service to his country, Cary High School, and my family.

The Rev. Connie Graddy and the members of the First United Metaphysical Chapel.

The administration, faculty, and students of Cary High School, the members of the Unification Church, and the management and employees of Shining Ocean for their prayers, love, and support.

The many gifted psychics and mediums that enabled me to communicate with my son.

Finally, a special word of thanks to the one who did more than anyone else to make this book possible, my wife and loving partner for twenty-seven years, Connie.

TABLE OF CONTENTS

INTRODUCTION

On August 11, 2003, I lost my 17-year-old first-born son to suicide. It's a tragedy that no one should ever have to go through, but I did, and I survived. I can't think of a more painful experience for a parent than having to bury a child.

Over thirty thousand people commit suicide in the United States every year. Some of those who are left behind do not survive the emotional and psychological shock waves that follow. Some sink into depression, some see their marriages and families break up, and some commit suicide themselves. It doesn't have to be this way.

This book recounts the details of the process my son and I went through before and after his death that took us on a path to healing, reconciliation, and peace. It is not just my story; it is his story as well. While my story transpires on this side of the veil of death, most of his is told from the "other side."

With the help of some gifted mediums, I was able to reestablish communication with my son after he died. The "letters" and other communication received from him are extraordinarily profound in the content they reveal. They describe what goes on in the mind of some suicides both before and after they end their lives. Also revealed is fascinating content about what suicides and others experience when they arrive on the "other side."

Through this process my son and I were carried from turmoil to calm, from guilt to forgiveness, from doubt to faith, and from separation to reunion. At various times along the way, we both had experiences that revealed the presence of a transcendent source of Divine love that dwells at the center of all reality.

I hope that this book will serve as a source of comfort to those who are going through what I went through. It is meant to provide assistance and hope to those who have lost loved ones, whether it is through suicide or some other cause. It is also a useful resource for young people to consider as they navigate the rocky waters of their teenage years.

Surprisingly, in the course of writing, I eventually realized that suicide is not the main subject of this book. My son's suicide became a catalyst that thrust me, and him, on a remarkable journey, and it is that journey that holds center stage. It was a journey of the spirit that I think anyone can relate to. It's a journey that began with shock, confusion, and anguish, but ended in discovery, reconciliation, hope, and joy. It's a journey that all of us in one way or another are traveling, one that involves the search for meaning in life and that demonstrates the central part love plays in it.

Along this journey, I experienced more fully the realization that life is spiritual at its core. We are eternal beings, and this life is a natural process of preparation for the next one, the one that begins when the physical body dies. I now see death as nothing to be feared, but as a normal part of our existence as natural and as exciting as a butterfly leaving behind the empty shell of its cocoon to spread out its wings and fly.

This book will take people to places no earthly person has ever seen before, and reveal things that most have never even imagined. It is a voyage of discovery. A father and a son, separated by death, reunited by love – this is our story.

PART I ASCENSION

1 YOGIC DISTURBANCE

"Is there a Mr. and Mrs. Pappalardo here?"
No one ever expects an armed police officer to barge into the middle of their yoga class and call out their name. Bewildered, the students and instructor gawked as my wife Connie and I, who were equally surprised, abandoned our yoga stretches and followed the officer's bulky form out the door into the bright sunlight. On that hot, muggy afternoon, as the cicadas buzzed in the trees, the officer from the Apex, North Carolina police department soberly handed me a slip of paper. Eyes diverted, he said, "There's been an accident back at your house; please call this number right away."

Connie's heart just about leapt through her t-shirt. I grabbed my cell phone, and in less than a minute, heard the familiar voice of Officer Bobby Beaman from the Cary Police Department; in recent months Bobby had graciously been helping us to navigate the complexities of raising a rebellious teenager.

"It's your son, Joshua," he said. "He's had an accident. It's pretty serious, but I think he's going to be okay."

"What kind of accident?" I asked.

After a pause on the other end of the line Beaman spoke: "He was burned."

2 SMOKE

Driving back to the house, my hands gripped the steering wheel tightly. I made a conscious effort to try and relax them. I appeared cool and calm on the outside, but inside my anxiety level was rising.

I'd lived in Cary, North Carolina since 1988 with my wife, Connie, and our four children. It was a tranquil suburb of the state capital, Raleigh. Cary is the closest thing to a contemporary version of Norman Rockwell's America that I know of. In the quaint downtown square, Ashworth Drugs boasts a popular old-fashioned soda fountain, and the Christmas parade that marches down Academy Street is still a big draw each year. It had been a great place to raise a family.

Native North Carolinians joke that Cary is an acronym for "Containment Area for Relocated Yankees." It's a fairly accurate description. Many Northerners moved here because of the excellent quality of life and the multitude of job opportunities. Cary's residents number more than 120,000—up from 25,000 when we first arrived – but it still has that old-time charm. It's consistently ranked one of the safest places to live in the United States, and a serious crime of any kind is still a rare event.

Yet, even in such an idyllic setting, there are pockets of that peculiar malady that plagues the human species – mental illness – and my family was not exempt.

As we pulled up to our house, Officer Beaman's car sat like a sentinel at the end of our normally quiet cul-de-sac.

"How's Josh?" I asked as I hurried up the driveway.

"He's already on the way to the hospital," said Beaman. "The EMS arrived very fast; they're taking him to the Jaycee Burn Center. The detective wants to talk to you for a few minutes, then you can head over to the hospital to see him."

"That's fine," I said, "just let me see how my other kids are doing first, okay?

Heading along the concrete path toward the front porch, I controlled a reflexive gasp as I noticed bits and pieces of charred clothing on the path and up the steps to the front door. Once inside the house, I was relieved to discover that my other children seemed stunned but composed. This was comforting, considering the circumstances. My daughter Nadia leapt up to hug me. We stood for a long moment, knit together in both love and somberness, before I asked as gently as I could, "What happened?"

My 12-year-old princess stepped back, took a deliberate breath, and began:

"I was down in the family room when the doorbell started ringing over and over. So I got up and opened the door and saw this guy standing there. I didn't recognize him. He looked really weird and there was smoke coming off his clothes. I thought he was some crazy homeless person."

Her eyes grew wider as she continued, "Then I realized, 'Oh my God! Josh, is that you?'"

The smoldering figure in front of her nodded in silent affirmation.

"Do you want me to call 911?" she asked urgently.

He gave another nod, then falling to his knees Josh sorrowfully uttered, "I'm sorry. I'm so sorry."

Nadia's words formed a scene of horror in my mind as I imagined what she had experienced only minutes earlier. Horror turned quickly into a terrible ache that, at such a young age, Nadia was the one who answered the door.

My 14-year-old son, Ariel, took up the narrative from his position near the couch: "Josh came inside and sat down over there," he said, pointing to the upholstered armchair in the living room. There were dark smudges on the chair, and as I approached I smelled a faint remnant of gasoline fumes drifting up from the fabric.

"Dad, his clothes were still smoking." I turned to hear my 15-year-old son, Gabriel, as he stood in the doorway to the dining room; he continued recounting the terrible event. "We called 911 and took him to the bathtub to try and cool him down. The EMS were here in like five minutes. They cut off some of his clothes with scissors, then they loaded him into the ambulance and were gone."

The children looked sad, but I could tell from their relatively calm demeanor that they weren't surprised. They knew that Joshua had suicidal tendencies, and, knowing their brother's melancholy disposition, they surrendered long ago to the fact that he might one day succeed. The three siblings not only accepted him, but also loved him deeply. This hadn't been his first suicide attempt; not two months had passed since he last tried to take his life. He had swallowed every pill he could find in the house one night, but the shock to his digestive system caused him to throw it all up before the chemicals could do their deadly work.

Concluding that the children seemed to be doing fairly well under the circumstances, I left them with Connie and sought the investigator. I found him outside in the yard waiting patiently.

"I'm Stephan Lampert," said the investigator. With calm authority he extended his hand in greeting and, without hesitation, asked if I had any idea who would want to harm my son.

"No sir, I don't," I replied quickly, taken aback by the question. The assertion that Josh may have had enemies became more understandable when the investigator asked if I could identify a gas can that they found in the woods behind my house. The police seemed to be speculating that some thugs jumped Joshua in the woods, poured gas on him, and lit him on fire with the intent to kill him.

Investigator Lambert led the way as we walked down a dirt path behind our house nestled between a creek on one side and beautiful old hardwood trees and Loblolly pines on the other. Along the way, I spotted more bits of charred clothing like those I had seen in the front yard. Like a trail of breadcrumbs, they led us to the grim scene.

Next to a large hardwood tree we found a gas can, or something that once resembled one. On the ground was a large gob of red plastic, melted into a mass that congealed into an unusable form. I was surprised to find it still hot to the touch. The sensation unexpectedly gripped me in a dreadful connection to the fire that engulfed my son. Escaping that terrible moment of reality, I forced my gaze up at the tree--the hardy companion who bore witness to the event. Ten feet and higher above my head, I was stunned to see leaves that were lush and green just an hour ago, were now charred to formless bits of black and gray, clinging weakly to their branches, a mirror image of Josh's burnt clothes clinging to his body.

Trying to make sense of the scene, my mind unconsciously attempted to recreate the event. The resulting image revealed my son encased in flames that seemed to reach for the heavens. I don't know if it's true or not, but someone later told me that gasoline burns at about 1500 degrees Fahrenheit.

All of this happened in a moment's time and I suddenly returned to the investigator discussing the ownership of the gas can. Even in its distorted shape, the gas can looked familiar. I told Investigator Lambert that it looked like mine, and he followed me to our back deck to confirm the guess.

As we returned along the path, my heart anguished to think of my first-born son, alone, running along this path back to the house with his clothes on fire. He was only seventeen. My thoughts strained painfully, "Oh, my boy. My poor boy!" I fought to get the image out of my mind and mustered all my strength to focus on the present.

We reached the deck and climbed the stairs to the place where I kept the gas can for my lawn mower. The empty space confirmed the awful suspicion.

I turned to Investigator Lambert and plainly stated what I knew in my heart to be true, "Detective, I really don't think there was anyone else involved in this. I think we've got a botched suicide attempt to deal with."

Just then, Connie opened the sliding glass door leading out to the deck. "I found this in Josh's room," she said holding up a sheet of notebook paper, the kind the kids use for school.

"What is it?" I asked.

"A suicide note."

3 TO THE HOSPITAL

As Connie and I drove to the hospital my mind was racing in a jumble of thoughts about what had happened and what might happen next. Speeding down Interstate 40, I wondered how serious Josh's burns might be, and what his chances of surviving might be.

"Do you think Josh is going to make it?" my wife of 21 years asked.

"I don't know, honey," I said. After a little more thought I muttered, "It might be better if he doesn't."

"What do you mean?" she said, surprised by my words.

"Well, if his injuries are severe and he survives, his suffering is just beginning. Burn injuries are some of the most painful injuries to recover from, and the path to recovery is long and hard. They have to do many surgeries for skin grafts and things like that."

Connie was quiet for a moment. "I hadn't thought about that," she said.

"On the other hand," I went on, "something like this will sometimes turn a life around. Sometimes when a person comes so close to death but survives, it's a wake up call. They suddenly realize that they want to live after all, and their attitude changes about a lot of things."

Another minute of silence went by, both of us lost in our thoughts. Then I remembered something.

"To be honest with you," I continued, "I don't think that's going to happen with Josh. He's never been much of a fighter. I don't know if he has what it would take to get through the ordeal.

"Do you remember that time Josh and I went whitewater rafting in the mountains in Pisgah National Forest? It was during the mini bootcamp for junior ROTC the summer before his freshman year." The Junior Reserve Officer Training Corps (JROTC) is a program that provides young people an opportunity to experience a taste of military life.

"Yes, I remember." Connie answered. "What about it?"

"Did I tell you how Josh got thrown out of the raft in the rapids?"

"Yes. You told me how you pulled him back into the boat."

"Well," I continued, "when that happened, it was really strange."

"What was strange?" Connie asked, her eyes turning away from the road ahead to look straight at me.

"I never told you this before, but when Josh fell into the river, he made absolutely no effort to get back into the raft. He just drifted there in the swirling water, with this weird smile on his face. It's like he had no desire for life in him."

4 BREAKING NEWS

The N.C. Jaycee Burn Center at the University of North Carolina Hospitals is known as one of the best–a world-class institution. I thought to myself, "If anyone can heal Josh from his injuries, these people can."

It takes about 40 minutes to get to Chapel Hill from Cary and we arrived in the early evening, about 7:30 p.m. It occurred to me that we are fortunate to have such a facility so close to where we live.

I had an eerie feeling walking in. The hospital is a big, big place. It was also very quiet–most employees had gone home for the day. We walked down corridor after corridor, passing cold, closed doors with various labels on them. We waited in silence at the elevator for a car to take us up to the floor that housed the burn unit.

You can't just walk into the burn center. You have to call in from a phone mounted on the wall near the locked entrance. This is understandable because doctors do all they can to prevent infection from entering the sterile area. Burn patients are highly susceptible to infection, so the staff doesn't want people just wandering in there spreading germs.

I picked up the phone and spoke to an attendant who said someone would come out to see us in a few minutes, and encouraged us to wait in the lounge down the hall.

We retraced our steps to the door that read Visitor's Lounge, and entered.

It was an antiseptic looking room with a few upholstered chairs, empty except for a modestly dressed middle-aged woman. I greeted her and asked where she was from.

She was from one of the rural counties west of Chapel Hill. Ironically, she was there for the same reason as us; her son had tried to kill himself. Like our son he had used gasoline, but he had done it inside the home where he was living alone, a singlewide mobile home. It burned to the ground.

I thought about Josh and flashed back to the scene at our house. What if he had done this in his bedroom, with the other children in the house? It suddenly occurred to me that we might have lost them all that afternoon.

The way she described him, this woman's son seemed to be frustrated and angry. Maybe he saw suicide as a way to get some sort of revenge on life, taking the house with him. In the ensuing inferno, even his dog had died.

Josh wasn't like that. He hadn't done this for revenge, or to hurt anyone, or out of rage. He was just suffering and wanted the pain to stop.

After his previous suicide attempt, Josh opened up to me a little, but didn't reveal many details.

"Dad, I should be dead, why am I still alive? I have really bad thoughts," he said. He believed that if people knew the kind of dark thoughts that flowed through his mind they would want him dead, too.

A year had passed since he was diagnosed with clinical depression. Joshua just wanted the mental torment to end, but he didn't mean to hurt anybody. The last words of his suicide note read, "I love everybody." I thought maybe this resulted in his choice to go into the woods, far away from the house.

"Mr. and Mrs. Pappalardo?"

We looked up to see two women standing in the doorway of the lounge, one in a nurse's uniform and the other dressed as a business professional.

"Will you come with us please?"

Connie and I followed the women down the hallway to the entrance of the burn unit where Josh lay. As we walked through the door, I noticed a hand washing station along the wall on my left. There was a sign indicating the dangers of infection to burn patients, and insisting that everyone wash their hands before going any farther. I walked over to the station but our escorts kept walking. "Shouldn't we wash our hands?" I called after them.

They stopped, turned around, looking a little confused.

"Sure," one of them said. "You can wash your hands if you like."

"If I like?" I thought to myself. "Why are they leaving this up to me?" Now I was the one confused.

After I washed up, we went around a corner into a conference room. As we each chose a seat around a large table, the women introduced themselves as a nurse and a chaplain.

"Dr. Peck, the head of the burn center, will be joining us shortly," said the nurse. "Your son is resting in one of the intensive care rooms, and you'll be able to go see him in just a minute. We just wanted to brief you on his condition and answer any questions you might have."

Connie was already getting a very bad feeling. First, she was pretty sure she knew why it didn't matter to either woman whether or not we washed our hands. Second, she was sitting across the table from a chaplain.

Just then, a distinguished-looking gentleman entered the conference room, wearing the garb of a physician. "Hi. I'm Michael Peck," he said, reaching out to shake my hand.

Dr. Peck exuded that air of confidence you get from men who are masters in their field–it's not at all arrogant, you just know this person excels at what he does. I began to feel more at ease. These three caregivers didn't have to say much before I felt their genuine warmth and concern.

I remember having read somewhere that the percentage of damage to the skin and the lungs is a deciding factor of whether or not a burn victim will survive. I cut to the chase. "Dr. Peck, before you go any further, I just want to ask one question if I might."

"Sure," he said gently. "Go ahead."

"What percentage of Joshua's body has suffered burns, and how are his lungs?"

He calmly answered without hesitation, "Ninety-seven percent, and not good."

"Wow," I thought to myself. "That's worse than I thought!"

I turned to Connie, touched her on the hand and said, "I'm sorry, honey, with burns that extensive there's nothing they can do."

There was a short silence. Nothing dramatic, just quiet resignation. Connie dropped her head and I could tell that she was beginning to cry.

For Connie and me the realization that our son was about to die was no surprise, though it didn't dull the throbbing ache of pain growing inside us. We thought Josh was making progress since his last suicide attempt, but you never know exactly what's going on inside a person's head–even that of your own son. Why did he choose today, the first day of the new school year, a day of hope and fresh beginnings for most students?

* * *

The night before, as Josh was getting ready to go upstairs to bed, I pulled out the last five dollars in my wallet and offered it to him.

"No, Dad, I don't need your money," he had said.

"Aw, go on, take it," I replied. "It's the first day of school. I want you to have a nice lunch."

I was surprised by his reaction. It was out of character for him to ever turn down money, but not enough to cause me to think he might be up to something. He finally took the money and went up to bed. It comforts me to know that my last words to him had been kind ones.

Our sympathetic doctor broke the silence. "I want to assure you that Josh is not suffering. We have him on medications for pain. We're keeping him comfortable."

"Dr. Peck, isn't there even a slight chance he might make it?" Connie asked.

"I don't think so, Mrs. Pappalardo. His injuries are so severe that his body can't handle the stress on so many systems at once. His heart will not be able to survive the strain of working to try to clear the fluid that is building up inside him."

"Can we talk to him?"

"I would encourage you to do so! Even though he won't be able to respond to you, there's a good possibility he'll be able to hear you. We've found that even when patients are unable to respond, they are still able to hear."

"How much time does he have?" I asked.

"Well, he's a strong young man. He'll probably be able to continue for about 18 hours."

"Can we see him now?"

"Sure."

5 DRIFTING AWAY

I was eager to see Josh, to let him know that we weren't angry with him for what he had done. His siblings noticed, when he came into the house after ringing the doorbell, he appeared very ashamed. As he sat in the big upholstered chair in the living room waiting for the ambulance to arrive, he asked his brother Ari to stop staring at him. "I'm really sorry," said Josh. "This is the stupidest thing I've ever done."

I needed to help him pass on knowing he was loved.

As Connie and I entered his room, the first thing I noticed were the bandages. His entire body had been carefully wrapped in sterile, white gauze so that only his face, fingertips, and feet were visible. He looked like an Egyptian mummy.

I was surprised to see that his face looked quite normal, and he seemed to be resting peacefully. He still looked as handsome as usual. His face bore the familiar summer look of someone with a little sunburn, perhaps a week old that had just begun to peel.

I was also surprised to find that the atmosphere of the room and the surrounding area was peaceful and bright. I think it had a lot to do with the caring staff members who dedicate themselves to the lives of those who enter the burn center. I felt such a sincere heart of concern coming from everyone, as though I was surrounded by angels.

The heart monitor above Joshua's bed revealed a more malevolent reality. What I saw there caused a queasy feeling in my gut. Even though Josh appeared to be quietly resting, his heart was pounding at more than 200 beats per minute. It was as if he was running full speed up a mountainside with every ounce of energy he had. A tube was running out of his mouth, and a small amount of an amber-colored liquid was slowly draining out. Although his face was serene, his body was fighting for its life, and it was losing.

"Hey, Joshie," I said, approaching the bedside.

"Hi, Baby," said Connie.

I moved closer so he could hear me. "Josh, I just want you to know that nobody's angry with you. We understand. I love you son, and I will always love you. Please don't worry."

"We forgive you Joshie," Connie said. "Please know that we will never stop loving you."

We stayed together there for a few more minutes, just comforting him, touching him, kissing him. Then I excused myself and asked to talk to the nurse.

"I know he doesn't have much time left. I'm wondering if I can use a phone to reach our children. I want to give them the opportunity to say goodbye to their brother."

"Of course," said the nurse.

Dr. Peck approached me and graciously offered the use of his office. Once again I was moved by the kindness and generosity shown to us.

I called the house and reached my 15-year-old son. "Gabe, your brother is alive, but they don't think he's going to make it. Do you have any message you'd like me to pass along?"

"Yeah, Dad," Gabriel replied. "Tell him that even though we fought sometimes there are no hard feelings, Okay? Tell him I'm not mad at him, and tell him I love him."

"Okay, son, I'll tell him right away. Now let me talk to Ari, okay?"

I was stunned at the level of maturity the children showed. I was afraid of someone going into hysterics, and wondered how I would handle it if they did. In hearing them express their love for their brother, I felt some of the weight lift off my shoulders. The other two expressed similar messages to Josh—we love you, we forgive you, don't worry about us.

Living with him the last few months had been a strain on everyone. Josh was a night owl, and would stay up eating popcorn and watching old movies because he couldn't sleep. We had a special drawer in the kitchen that had nothing in it except bags of microwave popcorn. It was hard for the other kids to sleep with their older brother banging around in the kitchen or using the bathroom while they all slept. It now appeared that those sleep-interrupted nights were about to become a thing of the past.

I went back to the room to check on Connie and Josh. Nothing had changed. The same serene atmosphere juxtaposed with the same ominous heart monitor racing at maddening speed was to be our temporary holding pattern.

All of a sudden, while sitting quietly with Josh, I began to realize I'd better prepare for what lay ahead. I needed to notify the authorities at Cary High to allow them adequate time to prepare to manage the emotional tidal wave about to hit the school. I went back to Dr. Peck's office to use the phone again.

I got in touch with Colonel Thomas Finnerty at his home. He was the retired Marine officer who headed up the Navy Junior Reserve Officer Training Corps program (NJROTC). I knew him well, and he knew Josh personally. I volunteered to be a van driver for the summer mini boot camp that Josh had attended as a rising high-school freshman. It was on that particular trip that Josh acted so strangely when he fell into the river while whitewater rafting.

I wanted to work closely with the school officials for a very specific reason. A few years earlier, another student had taken his life at Cary High, and within a few weeks several other students had taken their lives in copycat suicides. The phenomenon of suicides happening in clusters even has a name–the Werther effect–from a novel by Goethe.

"Col. Finnerty," I said over the phone, "Josh has attempted suicide–we're pretty sure he's not going to survive." I asked him to notify the high school principal.

"I'm so sorry to hear that, Mr. Pappalardo," he said sympathetically. We talked for a bit, and then I told him something I had wanted to say for years.

"Col. Finnerty, among the seemingly endless list of professionals Connie and I have worked with in our attempts to help Joshua deal with his problems, you have stood out like the morning star," I said. I continued, "Sir, I've been meaning to tell you this for a long time–I just want to let you know how much I appreciate your working with Josh, and the fine work you do with all the kids at Cary High. Men like you give me hope for the future of our country. I'm sorry Josh chose to not stay with the program. I think he would have been a lot better off if he had."

* * *

I sat for a while in Dr. Peck's office, lost in thought until a nurse appeared at the door.

She spoke gently, "Mr. Pappalardo, we think Joshua is in his final minutes."

I was taken by surprise. "How can that be? Dr. Peck said he'd live 18 hours," I thought to myself.

I ran to join Connie at his bedside. Josh's heart was still beating wildly; the contents of the tube oozing out of him had darkened.

Even as my son's life ebbed away, the atmosphere remained quiet and serene. I felt as if I was in the lobby of Heaven, and got the unexpected impression that I was witness to a sacred moment.

Josh's heart first began to slow. Then it stopped completely. He just quietly drifted away without a sound, like an autumn leaf falling gently and silently to the earth. It had been only about four hours since Josh arrived at the hospital. It was 11:10 pm, August 11, 2003. My 17-year-old son was gone.

PART II THE SEARCH

6 LIFE AFTER DEATH

When I was a boy it was said that you couldn't prove the existence of life after death because no one had ever died and come back to talk about it. That may have been true years ago, but events in recent decades challenge the old maxim.

People are living longer than ever before, and advances in medical technology have resulted in an increase in the phenomena of people being revived after reaching the point of being clinically dead.

In the 1960s a Swiss-born psychiatrist, Dr. Elisabeth Kubler-Ross, began in-depth studies of dying people. Unexpectedly, Dr. Kubler-Ross discovered that these patients often had unusual experiences in which they would describe crossing over into another world only to return with fascinating stories of their adventures on the other side. These episodes came to be known as near-death experiences, or NDEs.

Another psychiatrist, Dr. Raymond Moody, wrote a best-selling book in 1975 called *Life After Life* which compiled the experiences of over a hundred people who claimed to have had near-death experiences. To his amazement, Dr. Moody found that subjects described experiences remarkably similar regardless of age, ethnicity, or religious background. After observing these same elements repeated over and over again, he compiled a list of the common elements contained in a typical NDE.

I read Dr. Moody's book back in the mid-1970s and it made a profound impact on my thinking. I had been skeptical concerning the existence of a spirit world, and whether or not we were all destined to go there after physical death. The question of life-after-death became a favorite topic of my personal studies for decades, and I was always excited to discover and read new books on the subject. The result of this casual research and my own life experiences was a conviction that the human spirit does survive the death of the physical body. In my opinion, the body of evidence is overwhelming, and is growing all the time. My experiences after the passing of my son Joshua have simply strengthened this conviction.

7 ANGST

Connie and I returned home from the hospital, and the day had finally come to an end. I lay in bed imprisoned by my thoughts, "He's gone. He's really gone. I just can't believe this. How can this be happening?"

Now that Connie and I had joined the sad ranks of "devastated parents of children lost to suicide," I decided that looking out toward the future was better than looking in toward suffering endlessly in the past. Following that decision, an urgent sensation bubbled up through my troubled thoughts and suddenly two questions weighed on my heart that demanded immediate attention: Was Josh in peril on the other side? If so, was there something I could do from here to help him? I postponed the luxury of speculating about the whys and hows leading up to his suicide until I could answer these questions.

The inescapable fact was that, although my son was gone, he was still alive. He was still alive, but not on this material plane. I was sure that his spirit or soul must still exist somewhere. I needed to know what had become of him, and what kind of emotional state he was in. If there was any way to reach him and help him, I was determined to find it. I hadn't felt this sense of urgency when my parents died, but they had died after living a long life, from the ordinary failing of aging bodies, not a teenager who actively removed himself from this earth through the trauma of suicide.

Suicide was a subject that was never discussed in our family, nor in any families I knew. It was somewhat taboo, and I never knew anyone nor had I even heard of anyone who committed suicide.

The only information I gained was from my Catholic school education. The nuns taught us that suicide was a "mortal sin," the most severe classification in the theology of sin. A mortal sin was a spiritually fatal sin. They taught that murder and adultery were two others; as a result, the person who commits suicide was in pretty serious company. In other words if you purposely took your own life, you were damned to the fires of Hell for eternity.

As an adult, I was no longer a practicing Catholic, however, the teachings still hovered nervously in my subconscious. After Josh's death, I suddenly became worried. Maybe the nuns were right. Maybe Joshua is in Hell! The idea of my precious boy being consigned to eternal torment was more than I could bear. On the other hand, my heart cried out that it could not be so. Fear instilled during childhood is a powerful emotion, and there was a pretty potent dose of fear that accompanied my orthodox Catholic indoctrination.

Forcing my mind to settle down, I began to recall my more recent studies in the field of life after death. I believed that a more likely scenario was that Joshua was now in one of two possible places. So I examined these two possibilities one at a time.

The first possible state for Josh might be as an "earthbound spirit." An earthbound spirit is what becomes of a person who dies–loses his physical body–but for some reason remains on the earth instead of ascending into the spirit world. We've all heard of ghosts and poltergeists. These are two terms used for earthbound spirits.

Some spirits remain earthbound for a very simple reason–they just don't believe in life after death. Because they are incapable of accepting the possibility of surviving death in an immortal soul, they aren't open to the concept of ascending into the spirit world. Thinking they are still alive, they often just continue hanging out in their earthly neighborhood, oblivious to the world of spirit all around them.

In some cases, a homebuyer purchases a house in which a spirit continues to "live," and the unsuspecting homeowner unknowingly disturbs the earthbound spirit. From a ghost's point of view, the new owner is trespassing on private property, and the spirit does everything possible to get the intruder to leave. From this situation arises the phenomenon of the haunted house.

Other spirits remain earthbound because there is some unfinished business to attend to. An excellent rendition of an earthbound spirit is the guy who endlessly rides the New York subway trains in the 1990 movie *Ghost* that starred Patrick Swayze and Demi Moore. The actor Vincent Schiavelli portrays a spirit in denial of the fact that he has committed suicide, and tries to convince Patrick Swayze's character that he was pushed onto the tracks by some nameless adversary. This earthbound spirit would likely continue haunting the subway system until he can confront the issue of his suicide, or until he receives assistance from someone. For more on earthbound spirits, including suicides, see *Thirty*

Years among the Dead by Dr. Carl Wickland. So Josh might still be hanging around on the earth plane, lost and disoriented.

The second possibility is one in which the soul succeeds in ascending into the spirit world, but winds up in a place of darkness or confusion. In the case of a suicide, the spirit might be in an extreme state of emotional turmoil as he or she tries to come to grip with what has happened and all of its consequences.

This possibility resembles, in some ways, the concept of Purgatory, which in Catholic theology is a temporary place in which those destined for heaven receive due punishment for and cleansing of sins committed while on earth.

In either of these two scenarios, Josh would need help to ascend to a higher place in the spirit world. If I were to play any part in assisting him, I'd first have to figure out where he was.

8 LOST IN SPACE

The morning after Josh's death, I woke up feeling anxious. Imagine the feeling a NASA scientist might have if he woke up the morning after he had helplessly watched as one of his space exploration vehicles launched prematurely into the night sky. He knew it was out there, but he had no radio contact and no way to provide it with guidance. Josh was my little explorer, floating around somewhere in the spirit realms. What I needed was a "spirit radio" so I could make contact.

Several movies have been produced in recent years dealing with the spirit world, and although I don't agree with the exaggerated and sensationalized nature of some of the portrayals, there is some good material to be found in them, so I will continue to use a few of them here for illustrative purposes.

In 2005, Michael Keaton starred in a movie about a man who makes contact with the spirit world using something called Electronic Voice Phenomenon (EVP). The movie was called *White Noise*. EVP is a process by which people in the spirit world communicate with people on our earth plane using electronic devices. There is some remarkable documentation from scientists all over the world who have made contact with people in the spirit world using all sorts of electronic devices like telephones, tape recorders, and fax machines. This phenomenon is also known in the field as Instrumental Transcommunication (ITC).

I couldn't very well count on Josh to contact me, so I set out to find a method through which to contact him. I had learned that the easiest way to locate a spirit is to find a person who has the ability to perceive spirits without needing a device. I needed somebody like Haley Joel Osment in the movie *The Sixth Sense*, the kid who famously said, "I see dead people." The more I researched, the more I discovered that the number of people in the world who possess this perceptive ability must number in the thousands, perhaps even tens of thousands. Since Josh's passing, I've gotten to know many of these gifted people. At the time of Josh's passing, the only one I knew personally lived in Bellevue, Washington. So, the day after Josh died, I called Reverend David Hose.

9 THE MINISTER

The Rev. David Hose is not a typical minister, and he's not a typical psychic or medium either. I've known him for more than 30 years. The best way to understand this gifted human being is to hear part of his story.

David has a son who had always wanted a gun. David strongly opposed the idea, but while he was away for an extended period on mission work, the eager teen bought a .22 caliber rifle.

One day at dusk, the boy saw a deer snacking on the tender leaves on one of his mother's treasured apple trees. She spent a lot of effort tending the trees, and he thought she would be upset if the deer damaged the tree. Locating his rifle, he took a single shot into the semi-darkness and watched as something fell to the ground.

In one terrible moment, the boy realized that his mother had been on a stepladder pruning the tree, and what fell to the ground was not a deer. The bullet struck his mother's spine and, although she survived, she was rendered wheelchair-bound.

As a result of her injury, Mrs. Hose experienced severe episodes of muscle pain, with spasms moving uncontrollably through her back and legs. The anguish that the entire family has endured is heartbreaking.

In the midst of their suffering, David and Mrs. Hose didn't lose their faith in God. They cried out in prayer night after night from the depths of their hearts. One night as they prayed, and Mrs. Hose lay on the bed suffering in pain, David felt the presence of God in their bedroom. The presence carried with it a feeling of love that was as strong as a tidal wave. It pushed to make itself known, as if it had something it wanted to say, but David fought the sensation, and the presence left.

The second visit from this compassionate presence brought with it even stronger sensations of love. This time, David surrendered to the benevolent force, and as his wife lay on the bed in agony, he opened his mouth and spoke. The voice was his voice, but the words were coming from somewhere else. The words conveyed an overwhelming love, a deep compassion the likes of which the couple had never experienced. The two of them were overcome with tears of gratitude and bathed in an all-encompassing parental love coming from a spiritual source.

David told me what a blessing is was to have this once-in-a-lifetime encounter with the living God. They would forever be transformed by the memory of this unique experience.

Another day, the Hoses discovered that it wasn't a one-time blessing. It happened again—and then again. Over the course of the next few years, the Hose's experienced literally dozens of these messages from God, and began recording them on audiotape as they happened. Eventually, they built a collection of messages and published some of them in a book called *Every Day God*.

10 AFTERMATH

I was aware that David could contact God, but I didn't know that he also had the power to directly contact lower spirits. Even though he had the ability to contact spirits like Josh, he didn't tell many people about it, including me, because he wasn't interested in talking to anybody in the spirit world except–as David put it–"the Guy in charge." Knowing this, I contacted him only for a referral. I knew that in the process of publishing his book he had met a lot of interesting people with various psychic gifts and mediumship abilities, and I was hoping he could steer me in the right direction.

David recommended a woman near Seattle named Barbara Ten Wolde. He informed me that she was about to depart for an extended overseas trip and to call her right away to ask for her help. I called her as soon as we finished talking, only to reach an answering machine. Disappointed, I left an urgent message and hung up.

With my plans temporarily thwarted, I returned to the pressing issues at hand–dealing with the emotional fallout at Cary High School and making plans for Joshua's memorial service.

***

I called to make an appointment to see Dr. David Coley, the principal at Cary High School, and he offered to see me right away. As a man-with-a-mission to do the right thing—a perfectionist habit of mine—I drove to the school, entered through the administrative building, and continued on to the counselors' offices. As I came through the second door, I saw a room full of students waiting to talk to their counselors. In the chair closest to the door sat a young lady of about seventeen. Her tear-stained cheeks and red, puffy eyes revealed the depth of heartache I suspected I might see in the eyes of many who knew Josh and had just learned of his death.

My heart ached for this girl and I couldn't help but go to her side and comfort her as best I could. I had shelved my own grief to assist others in their suffering, partly out of a sense of responsibility and partly due to a total loss of knowing what to do at all.

When I asked her what was wrong, she responded through stuttering breath, "A friend of mine just died, and it's got me really upset."

"What was your friend's name?"

"Josh Pappalardo," she said.

"Well, then you ought to give me a hug, cause I'm his daddy."

She immediately stood up, threw her arms around me, and started to cry. I just held her gently for a minute while she let her grief pour out. As she slowly calmed down she drew her arms away and spoke.

"Josh was one of my best friends," she said. "Whenever I was feeling down he would flash me that mischievous grin of his and it always made me feel better. I can't believe he would do this. I came here 'cause I just needed to talk to somebody about it, and they said we could come and talk to the counselors.

"Josh was such a good friend. He would always take the time to listen to me whenever I had a problem. When he listened, he would look right at you–you could tell he really cared."

Her eyes started to well up again.

I encouraged her to talk with the counselors and followed up with an open invitation to our home.

"For real?" she asked incredulously.

"Absolutely!" I answered. "We've opened the house to anyone who wants to come over and just hang out and be together. Some of Josh's other friends have already visited."

"Thank you so much, Mr. Pappalardo. I'll do that after school. Josh never told me he had such a cool dad," she said with a sheepish grin. That didn't surprise me. With the confrontations I had with Josh in the last couple of years, I doubt he thought of me in terms of being cool.

Upon leaving the student waiting room I walked to Dr. Coley's office. He received me with genuine sympathy and asked me how I was doing. I told him that I wanted to do anything I could to help the students get through this, and that my biggest concern was to avoid copycat suicides.

"I'm really grateful that the media hasn't sniffed the story out yet," I said, breathing a sigh of relief.

I cringed to imagine what the television reporters might do if they caught wind of the news–"Cary High student commits suicide after first day back at school." They would badger the administration, teachers, and students with questions. They would set up their cameras in front of the school and broadcast the footage in every half-hour news segment for a couple of days. They would dredge up the old stories of earlier suicides of Cary High students, and then the inevitable would happen–copycats. I had already seen the copycat phenomenon once, and I prayed to God it wouldn't happen again.

I suggested to Dr. Coley that we continue to keep things low-key, and maybe we could stay under the media's radar.

"I think you're doing the right thing by encouraging the students to visit their counselors if they need to," I said. "I'm not expecting the school to make announcements or hold a service for Josh. In fact I hope you don't. The less we publicize this, the less we inadvertently encourage other students to imitate him. It is also less likely that anyone will leak the news to the media. Our family is offering a memorial service that will be completely open to anyone who wants to come– students, faculty, anybody." I repeated my invitation that anyone who desired could come out to the house to visit, pray, talk, or whatever they needed to do to deal with Josh's death.

11 FIRST GLIMPSE

"David Hose just called," Connie said as I came in the door, returning from the high school. "He said you should call him right away."

My heart beat faster as I went to the telephone. I looked forward to any news about Josh.

"Hello, Ron," said the familiar voice on the line from Seattle. "I just got off the phone with Barbara Ten Wolde."

I held my breath.

"She wasn't able to talk to Josh," David continued, "but she was able to locate him in the spirit world."

"Where is he?" I implored.

"Well, it's kind of a transition place. She saw him standing in a pool of some kind of liquid–like water, but not water. She could see him from the waist up, and he wasn't wearing a shirt," David replied.

"There were some type of spiritual beings glowing with a bright light at the pool with him, and they were reaching into the liquid, and very slowly and gently pouring it over his body, soothing him."

"That's great!" I nearly shouted into the phone.

"But she wasn't able to talk to him, Ron. It's too soon. She said to give it a few days, after he's had some time to settle in."

I was ecstatic. These were excellent signs. Josh had not descended into a dark place, which I thought might likely be the case given his emotional state. For whatever reason, he was in a good place, and the entities that were ministering to him, which might be angels or other spirit men, were clearly on the side of the light, not darkness.

I finally spoke to Mrs. Ten Wolde directly a couple of days later, but she just repeated what David communicated earlier–it was too early to talk to Josh.

12 SPLASHED

When a teenager dies, the memorial service is usually a crowded event. The whole community expresses a great deal of sympathy and support for the family, and ours was no exception. My employer graciously gave me as much paid time off as I needed, and a collection from the employees and other kind people raised enough money to cover all of Josh's final expenses. Some of the people who helped us were total strangers. Some had also lost a teenager and sympathized with us during our time of distress.

Connie and I decided to rent the largest chapel at the funeral home we were working with to accommodate all who might attend. We also planned an unusual service. The intention was to make it a celebration of Josh's life. I hoped that the atmosphere would be bright and uplifting, rather than mournful and somber. My intuition told me that it would be helpful for Josh if we did things in a more positive spirit.

I had never experienced working with a funeral home before. I had always thought they were kind of creepy, and I thought that anyone who would agree to work in one must have been desperate to find a job. My feelings toward funeral workers evaporated after working with the people who managed Josh's affairs. I discovered that many of the people in this industry felt a calling to work there–to some it was a form of ministry, no less of a commitment than being pastor of a church.

The funeral counselor that helped us plan the memorial service, Donnie Collier, was one such person. I could see that his job was more than just a livelihood–he sincerely concerned himself with my family, and me in particular. When I began explaining to him what happened, I suddenly began to weep uncontrollably. I put my head on the shoulder of this total stranger and, like a brother, he just held me while I felt the sting of my son's death fully for the first time.

As the grief ebbed, like a wave returning to the sea, we began to discuss preparations.

I asked Donnie if it would be all right if I led the service myself. I had served as pastor for churches in the past, so conducting a service wasn't something foreign to me, although I had never presided over a memorial service, much less one of a member of my family.

"Sure you can," Donnie said supportively. He hesitated for a moment before continuing, "But while you've been taking care of everything up to this point, and while at the service you'd be ministering to everyone else, who's going to take care of you?"

The comment hit me like a splash of cold water. He was right. I had been in a state of manic activity since the moment the police officer appeared at the yoga studio, and the stress was starting to show.

"Mr. Pappalardo," he continued, "you are welcome to do things however you like, and we are here to support you, but I think it would be better if you find someone you trust that can share some of this burden with you."

I didn't know what to say.

"I'll think about it," was all I could muster.

13 ODYSSEY

Driving back to the house from the funeral home in Raleigh, I began to weigh Donnie's words. I knew it would be best if I could find someone to help me with the memorial service, but trying to figure out whom to ask was a challenge.

Although both Connie and I were raised Roman Catholic, we were not practicing Catholics, so calling the local parish priest was out of the question.

When my wife and I were 20-years-old we joined the Unification Church of Sun Myung Moon, which is where we met. In a highly publicized event, more than 2000 couples were married at the famous mass wedding ceremony that was held in Madison Square Garden in New York on July 1, 1982. We were one of those couples.

In 1995, both of us concluded that it was time for us to search elsewhere for spiritual nourishment—our experience with the Unification Church had become dry. After some "church shopping," we settled in with a Pentecostal congregation. The pastor was trying to help people nurture their own direct relationship with God, which we found appealing. Unfortunately, he got "burned out" and quit after we had been there for a few months, the focus changed, and we decided to move on.

Later we joined a Baptist church at the behest of 12-year-old Joshua. Our whole family was baptized together and Joshua and Gabriel joined the youth group. It was a noble and sincere endeavor, but the net result was a disappointment. The congregation fought over the direction proposed by the new pastor; he was eventually dismissed in a bitter recall vote. The doctrine seemed centered around fear and guilt instead of the love of God. Eventually, we just kind of drifted away.

We needed to locate someone we were comfortable with to preside over Josh's service, but our options were few.

The Unificationists still welcome us as part of their community; we established lifelong friendships there with some of the most beautifully spiritual people you could ever want to meet. We could have requested a

Unificationist ceremony, but it wouldn't have felt right. Joshua and our other three children never embraced the Unificationist faith.

Catholic? Unificationist? Baptist? None of these seemed like good options. Back to square one.

14 HOUSEKEEPING

School had let out by the time I got back to the house, and the place looked like Grand Central Station in New York. Teenagers were everywhere–on the front steps, in the living room, in Josh's bedroom, walking in the woods. This was a phenomenon that was non-stop during the days surrounding the memorial service. It's also something for which Connie and I were really grateful. We've always loved having teenagers in the house. Their youthful energy and big appetites–spiritually as well as physically–kept us busy and our spirits up.

One of our dear friends from our Unification Church days did something for which we are eternally grateful. Gayle Davis just felt in her heart that we needed her help, told her husband she'd be gone for a few days, and basically came over and became part of our family for a week. She relieved Connie of all her household duties and served us in so many other ways. I don't know how we would have survived without her. She truly exemplified the spirit of true religiosity. As the saying goes, she didn't just "talk the talk," she "walked the walk."

The teenagers just kept on coming. As soon as one group would leave, another group would arrive. We fed them, comforted them, and spoke with them. I told them I thought Josh was still alive–he just wasn't alive here anymore. Some of them didn't believe it, some of them wanted to hear more. These discussions went on for hours.

"Mr. Pappalardo, is it okay if we hang out in Josh's room for a little while?" some would shyly ask.

"Sure," I would reply. "Stay as long as you need."

I did something else that is still controversial with my children–I gave away a lot of Josh's stuff. I allowed his friends to take things from his room if they wanted something to remember him by–things like his punk rock band posters, t-shirts, Final Fantasy action figures. It just felt like the right thing to do.

I had several thoughts surrounding this cleansing action. I thought it might help Josh let go of the material world and focus on his new life.

Second, I preferred that his things wound up with people that would cherish them instead of seeing them disposed of or sold at a yard sale. Third, I knew that it would spare Connie and me the anguish of having to sort it out ourselves, dealing with all the emotions attached to these things.

A few really close friends insisted I lead them to the spot where Josh had doused himself with gasoline. At first I said no, but their persistent requests led me to give in, and I took them there. A couple of them knelt down for a moment of silence.

Fortunately, the place did not become a shrine. I was still worried about copycats. I allowed Joshua's room to be the shrine. That way, I had some control over what was going on. I didn't divulge the location of his self-immolation to others who asked for it.

A few of Josh's friends told me they were upset that the high school wasn't doing anything special to honor Josh's memory.

"It's not fair," they said. "One of the athletes got killed in a car crash and they made a big deal out of it, but they're not doing anything for Josh. They just didn't like Josh and the people he hung out with."

I explained that the school had done nothing wrong, and that I had actually asked that things be kept low-key to avoid the risk of copycat suicides. Some didn't seem very convinced.

Later, I met again with some school officials and we decided that at the end of classes on Friday, just before school let out for the weekend, there would be an official announcement. Afterwards, I asked the students about the announcement.

"It was very nice, Mr. Pappalardo," one of them told me. "They expressed their condolences to 'Josh's family and friends' and announced the memorial service–they said everybody was welcome to come."

Somehow, the press never got a hold of the story, and to my great relief, there wasn't a single copycat suicide.

At some rare, quiet moment, I got a chance to talk to Connie about what had happened at the funeral home.

"Donnie Collier, the funeral director, thinks it would be better if I have someone else lead the service, but I don't know who to ask," I told her.

"Why don't you ask David Hose to come and preside over the service?" she suggested. "He's not a traditional Unification Church member, and he understands our situation probably better than anyone else."

"But he's in Seattle," I responded. "Do you think he would come here all the way from Washington?"

"Why don't you just ask him and see?" she replied.

15 RESCUED

When I reached David Hose on the phone it was a bad time for him. He sounded like he had a lot of things going on. He said he'd have to look at his schedule and get back to me before he could give me an answer–I was surprised at how disappointed I felt.

The human psyche is so complex, especially under stressful situations. During this period, I don't think I knew what I was really feeling on a conscious level. I just kept moving forward, sensing that the worst thing to do would be to stop and think about all that had happened. I was grateful for the stream of visitors–most of them teenagers–that kept showing up on our doorstep. It was a blessing to be able to take care of them.

I had an experience in my twenties that convinced me that I would never have problems slipping into depression if I was serving someone else. It seems to work like magic every time I try it. The experience took place in Boulder, Colorado. I was living in a pyramid-shaped Unification Church center across the street from the University of Colorado. It was like a coed monastery. Imagine about 40 twenty-somethings living together like monks and nuns. Dating was not allowed, and everyone treated each other as a brother or sister. It was a beautiful experience.

One day, I fell into a strange mental state, feeling down and doubting my faith and struggling with the idea of leaving the church. I retreated to the chapel, where I brought the matter to God in prayer. I prayed and prayed but found no relief. I told God I was going to stay in the chapel until I either dropped dead or this strange state of mind passed from me.

After a few hours in the chapel, I suddenly felt an inspiration to go downstairs to the dining hall. When I arrived, I found a guest sitting alone at a table. I thought to myself, "This poor fellow, nobody's taking care of him."

I greeted the guest, and offered to get him something to drink. Moving to the kitchen, I made the guest a cup of tea, carefully adding the milk and sugar so it wouldn't spill. I returned to the guest, gently placed the cup and saucer on the table, and returned to the kitchen. As I walked away from the guest, I stopped in mid-stride.

"Oh, my God," I thought. "The feeling's gone."

I came to the conclusion that because I had forgotten about myself and focused on the needs of someone else, the dark mental state lost its hold on me. I returned to the guest and listened to him pour out his heart, which is something that happened a lot in Unification Church centers in those days. Afterwards, I was as good as new again.

David Hose called me back a couple of hours later. "Yes, I will come," he said with a determined tone in his voice. "Just tell me where I need to be, and I'll be there."

Immediately, I choked up and started to cry. Trying to talk to David through my sobbing, I thanked him profusely, and told him I would make all the travel arrangements and get back to him. A huge feeling of burden lifted from me.

Again, I was surprised by my emotional reaction. Since my parents' death, David was the closest thing to a father figure that I had in my life. I truly felt like my dad was coming to save the day, and I wouldn't have to shoulder all the weight myself anymore. It was such a relief.

That night I slept a lot better.

16 BIRTHDAY

The next few days were filled with visitors, which made the situation infinitely more bearable. Joshua had passed on from the physical life on Monday; the memorial service was scheduled for Sunday. Somehow, I was able to find a reasonably priced plane ticket that got David to Raleigh-Durham airport in good time. If I remember correctly, the airline gave us a discounted rate because David was flying in to preside over a funeral.

The next problem to solve was perplexing. Friday, August 15, would be my second son Gabriel's 16th birthday. How do we celebrate a birthday in the midst of sadness?

Gabe had been a real trooper. He went to school the very next day after Josh died and did an impressive job comforting friends and being our family's ambassador to everyone he came in contact with.

He had just lost his older brother, the person he grew up with playing Teenage Mutant Ninja Turtles–he was Donatello to Joshua's Leonardo, and the Mario Brothers–he was Luigi to Joshua's Mario– running around the house in green overalls and a baseball cap. We didn't want him to lose his birthday, too.

Once again, the community came to the rescue. One of Gabriel's high school buddies suggested we have a surprise party for Gabe at his house. The parents endorsed this proposal wholeheartedly, and even insisted on taking care of all the details–birthday cake, pizza, etc.

We fooled Gabriel into thinking he was just going over to Ryan's house to help him with homework. Surprise! Ironically, it turned out to be the best birthday Gabriel had ever had.

PART III CONTACT

17 BREAKTHROUGH

Sunday came, and the house was a zoo. Friends, high school kids, and neighbors swarmed, it seemed, over every inch of the house. My boss and a coworker flew in and graciously offered to chauffeur us to the service. David Hose's plane had come in the night before, and he slept in the family room downstairs. The house was overflowing with food, flowers, and messages of condolence.

A few hours before the service was to start, David came to me with a nervous look on his face.

"Ron," he said. "The service is at 3:00 and I haven't finished composing my talk yet. Have you got a quiet room where I could go to collect my thoughts?"

I looked into the living room–it was packed with guests. I knew it would be the same scene in the family room.

"What do I do now?" I thought. "I don't want to kick people out, but David needs some space." Then it occurred to me that there was one place in the house that was very quiet–Joshua's room–but I thought David might be a little hesitant to go in there.

"David, would you feel comfortable using Joshua's bedroom? Right now, that's the only quiet place in the house."

"Sure," David replied enthusiastically. "That'll do just fine."

"It's the door in the back up there," I said, pointing to the upper floor of our split-level house.

"Thanks, Ron." With that, he bounded up the stairs with his pen and pad in hand.

A few minutes later, he stuck his head out the door and called to me.

"Hey Ron, could you come up here?"

Puzzled, I climbed up the stairs to Josh's room. David had closed the door behind him after calling to me, so I slowly opened it and stepped in. I found David kneeling very quietly on the floor. It seemed that he might be crying.

"Ron, Joshua is here in the room right now," he said.

I stopped breathing. Stunned, I couldn't find anything to say for a moment. David was just sitting there motionless, in deep concentration. I could see the tears now on his cheeks.

"David, are you able to communicate with him?" I asked anxiously.

"I don't know. Give me a minute."

The minute seemed like an hour. Finally David broke the stillness.

"He's in a lot of emotional distress right now, but I think–if we give him time–I think he has something he wants to say."

After another long moment passed, David spoke again–but he wasn't talking to me.

"Josh," he said, "In a couple of hours we're holding a memorial service for you. Is there anything you want to say to your friends?"

Another quiet pause, and then, David's voice gently broke the silence.

"He spoke," David said, his voice almost a whisper. "Just four words … very slowly. 'Don't…ever…do…this!'"

I opened the door and called for Connie to come up. After she joined us, Josh began to speak through David a little more. He seemed hesitant at first, as if he wasn't sure if he was even welcome in our house anymore. He was feeling a tremendous amount of shame and guilt, worried that he had deeply disappointed us. After a while I grabbed a legal pad and began to take notes. Unfortunately, I didn't get everything down. A lot of what Josh said has been lost, but here are some of the things I wrote on the legal pad. At first it seemed he was responding to David's question; if he had been given a chance to speak directly to his teenage friends, this is what he would have wanted to say. The time was 12:40 p.m., August 17, 2003:

"I'm not gone."

"Don't forget me. I'm still here."

"You should know there's something beyond this life. I'm not saying you should go back to church, but you should live your life with the understanding that there's more to it after you die."

This was typical Josh. He had really soured on institutional religion, after having had some disappointing experiences.

"Dad, you have to tell my friends this–your clothes, what you wear, or whether or not you're popular doesn't mean shit!"

Anyone who knows David Hose knows that he is the last person in the world who would have expressed himself like this. When I heard the word "shit"–one of Josh's favorite expressions–I said to David, "Now that really sounds like Josh."

Immediately Josh replied, "You can quote me on that." I couldn't help myself, and I laughed. What a bizarre situation. My son has committed suicide, and here I was sitting on the floor of his bedroom talking to him through spirit communication, laughing because he said the word "shit." They never covered this in Parenting 101.

David said that Joshua had a strong feeling of regret, a feeling of failure.

We comforted him and told him we loved him and weren't angry with him.

By this point we were joined by Gabriel and Ari. Nadia still hadn't emerged from her bedroom.

Again through David, Joshua said, "Tell Nadia I love her."

The last thing I wrote down was a question from me to Josh.

"Could you hear us when we were talking to you in the hospital room?"

"I couldn't hear your words at the hospital, but I could feel them. I could feel the love. Right now I can hear you really well."

This session with Josh lasted about 20 minutes. At the end, Joshua mentioned some beings from the other side that were trying to communicate with him.

"There are some people who want me to go with them. They seem like they're good, but I don't know any of these people."

I encouraged Josh to go with these entities. I thought they would escort him to a good place in the spirit world. This appeared to be a classic experience of a somewhat earthbound spirit. In many other instances, the deceased will recognize familiar faces on the other side, such as parents, grandparents, or friends who have gone on before them. I was surprised that Josh couldn't recognize any of the spirits who were beckoning him, and didn't know what to make of it. I thought it might be because there weren't many people he knew who had gone to the spirit world before him. His grandparents had both crossed over when he was very young, and he didn't know them that well. They lived in Florida and we only managed to make a handful of visits before they passed on.

It also seems that many spirits will not ascend until after their memorial service. The service seems to play an important role in their ascension process.

Josh eased my mind when he finally said, "I'll probably go with these guides eventually."

He concluded with a simple housekeeping comment, addressed primarily to his siblings.

"Don't fight over my stuff; whatever you want to do with it is okay."

With that, the communication ended.

18 BOOSTER ROCKETS

We arrived an hour early at the funeral home, and already there were a couple dozen teenagers waiting in the parking lot. Many were wearing black, and some had been crying. Ironically, I was in a great mood. As strange as it may sound, I had just had the most heartfelt conversation with my son that I had had in a long time, and I felt very good about it.

As Josh struggled more and more with his depression, he became increasingly distant. It was quite an accomplishment if you could get him to say more than a sentence to you in any conversation. So, talking with him for 20 minutes was just wonderful for me.

A typical conversation with Josh was like the last one I had with him while he was still physically alive. Oddly, coming home from school, he had entered the house from the rear through the sliding glass doors in the dining room. My guess is it had something to do with the fact that the gasoline can was stored on the outside wooden deck. Connie and I happened to be standing there in the dining room when he came in. Without saying a word he just walked past me towards the stairs.

"Joshua, how was your first day at school?" I asked him.

"It sucked."

"What about drama class? How was drama?"

"It sucked, too," he repeated as he bounded up the stairs. We had hoped that getting him into drama class, something he seemed to enjoy, would be a bright spot in his high school experience.

Before he disappeared into his room his last comment was a typical one. "It all makes me wanna puke," he said before closing the bedroom door behind him.

Those were the last words he said to me before he died. It was right after this that we left for our yoga class.

I asked Donnie Collier, the funeral director, if we could let the guests come in early, and he happily obliged. Before 30 minutes had passed, the chapel was packed with over 200 people. By the time the service started, it was standing-room only.

This was going to be an unusual service by traditional standards. For one thing, none of us in the family were wearing black. For another thing, there was no casket–we decided to have Josh cremated. The only object in the front of the chapel was a large, framed copy of Josh's high school yearbook photo, surrounded by the beautiful flowers that had been sent. There was no somber music. Josh loved to go with the whole family every autumn to the Renaissance Fair in the countryside near Charlotte, so we chose a beautiful collection of Celtic music for the prelude.

There was a reason we arranged things this way. My goal for having the memorial was twofold:

First, I wanted the energy to be high and uplifting. Going back to the analogy of the NASA scientist with his prematurely launched space exploration vehicle, I saw positive energy as adding a couple of extra booster rockets to Josh's ascension. (Later events would validate my intuition.) We parents usually try our best to help our kids however we can. This was one thing I could do from this side of the veil to help my son transition to his new life.

Second, I wanted to give Josh's fellow students, friends, and family an opportunity to directly participate. I felt this would be a good way for them to be able to move forward after such a traumatic event in their lives. I hoped the atmosphere would be less like a traditional funeral and more like a big family reunion.

We kept some traditional aspects by printing up programs and having some structure, and Rev. Hose gave a moving eulogy. But the part I was most interested in was the time that we allowed for people who knew Josh to express themselves.

They did so in several different ways. Joshua's guitar teacher gave a hard-rockin' performance of a song dedicated to his young student. A high school girl composed a beautiful poem in his honor. Then we just opened up the microphone to anyone who wanted to say something.

As Connie and I sat in the front row, closely watching these precious young people tell their stories, we were awestruck by the deep affection so many of them had for our son. We had no idea he was so beloved, and I speculated that he must have had no idea how loved he was either.

Student after student emphasized one thing over and over again– that Josh was a good listener, that he invested a lot of time paying attention to his friends as they shared their thoughts, their problems, and their various moods. So many of them mentioned the powerful effect his smile could have on them, and how he would just flash that smile or laugh to lift them up when they were down and struggling with the various challenges associated with being a teenager.

The "open mic" portion of the service went on for quite some time, probably longer than some of the adults would have liked, but I thought it was really important.

Then Connie and I were further surprised when our children, without any prodding from us, one by one took the microphone to share their hearts. Once again I was dumbfounded. How could they act so mature at such a young age? How could they so understand what their brother had gone through?

The students and friends had seen the very best attributes of Joshua's personality, but we family members who lived with him got to see the results of the darkness that plagued his mind. It was sometimes terribly disturbing–our family had been through a lot. I was really surprised and grateful to see that the children were handling it so well.

19 SÉANCE

Back at the house, we were again inundated with students, friends, and other well-wishers. Connie confided that at the time she felt guilty at how much genuine fun she was having. The last group didn't leave until midnight.

One of them was Josh's ex-girlfriend and her best friend who also loved Josh a lot. David told them he was going to try and get in touch with Josh in the morning, so we invited them over for breakfast.

They showed up on our doorstep with a third young lady around 7:00am.

We sat around talking and munching down eggs, bagels, and other assorted breakfast fare, marveling at how well the service had gone. Watching the scene, no one would ever have guessed that a séance was about to take place.

There were no candles, crystal balls or anything at all out of the ordinary, just a bunch of friends eating, gabbing away, and enjoying each other's company.

After we finished, David asked us to join him in a prayer. We bowed our heads, and David uttered a prayer asking for God to hear us, to grant that his Holy Spirit might be present, and guide our fellowship.

Then he fell silent–so did everyone else. It was so quiet you could hear a pin drop. After a moment, he spoke. His voice was so soft I could barely hear him, but it was somehow very clear what he had just said: "Josh is here with us."

I had already prepared by bringing my legal pad and pen. As Josh spoke to us through the instrument of David's psychic gift, this time I got everything almost exactly as it was spoken.

Unlike the hesitant, uncertain Josh from before the service, this Josh spoke much more clearly and, this time with a measure of hopefulness we hadn't seen the day before.

The message was short and succinct; nevertheless it was quite profound and complete.

We later made copies and gave it to anyone who was willing to receive it. It is presented here just as I wrote it down that day.

Morning of August 18, 2003:

I want to express my thanks for all the love I received yesterday. It's not so easy for me to come right now because I have to make some adjustment, but it seems that because of all the love that's around me I'm given this opportunity to express the gratitude I feel with all the overflowing love I experienced from you yesterday.

It's clear that I was surrounded by your love and the love of God. I should have been more sensitive to the way you felt about me when I was with you.

I think I've already learned something because being here makes things very clear. Thank you for your great love.

I stand here to wish you the best as you go on your journey, as I go on mine.

Don't waste time listening to the buzzing in your head. Do you understand? You know, the waves of negative thoughts that go on inside your head? I've learned I must rise above that.

I'm in no position to give advice, but I want to say something more deeply than just "Don't ever do this." Please don't give in to those negative emotions. You are too precious to give in to those things.

All the help you need for your life is right there with you, on earth. You just have to look around you so you can see it. Your friends, your family... they're all there to help you.

Again, thanks. You helped me powerfully yesterday. Sometime soon I can be more free maybe. I want to be in contact with you, because you are the best people I know.

20 FRIENDLY ADVICE

Needless to say, I was just amazed by this message. I knew that Joshua wasn't out of the woods yet, but I could see that he was well on his way. I suspected that he was beginning to accept help from his guides, and would continue to do so. I was really curious to know who these spiritual beings were, but I wouldn't find out until much later.

The thing that made me the happiest was at the end when he said, "You helped me powerfully yesterday."

The whole situation of Josh's depression and suicide had left me in a state of deep anguish. As parents of a suicide, it is probably inevitable to struggle terribly with self-doubt and a profound sense of failure–"Why wasn't I able to protect my son from this tragedy? Why didn't I do something differently? There must have been something more I could have done to prevent this!"

As someone who has been through it, I would caution others not to dwell on these thoughts. Let them come into your consciousness and acknowledge them, observe them, and then let them go again like a leaf that slowly drifts by you in an autumn breeze. Let it go. Don't pick it up to get a closer look. Just let it go.

Recognize that there is a Higher Power present in your life, and let negative thoughts go by. If you dwell on them, they are very destructive. They can destroy your own sanity, your marriage, and your family. Cultivate humility, a humility that recognizes that you can't control everything. You do your best and leave the rest in the hands of God.

Also, cultivate forgiveness. If you feel that others have failed your loved one in some way that led to the suicide, it's all right to entertain that thought–it might even be true. You must nevertheless forgive them, and if you think that you have failed your loved one, you must forgive yourself as well. If you are having a hard time forgiving, ask for the ability to forgive, and you may receive it.

One thing that helps me forgive is thinking about someone who had a more difficult situation than me, and yet found a way to forgive anyway. If you still have a hard time forgiving, maybe this will help. Imagine Jesus hanging on the cross, his life slowly ebbing away from him as he bleeds from multiple wounds. He's having a hard time even breathing. He looks down at those who are executing him. In that tragic situation, an innocent man being killed in a brutal fashion, it would have been understandable if he had expressed bitterness, anger, or a desire for revenge. It never fails to move my heart when I consider that instead he raised his voice to heaven and prayed for his tormentors–"Father forgive them; for they know not what they do." (Luke 23:34 RSV) If he could forgive in such an extreme situation, I can forgive in mine.

Be honest about your feelings. It's okay to feel the way you do. They are valid feelings. Talk to someone about them, acknowledge them, but don't dwell on them. Again, I believe that if you focus on the needs of others around you, you won't fall into depression.

Humility, forgiveness, and honesty are powerful tools for you to use to get through the turmoil.

When Josh said, "You helped me powerfully yesterday," I felt tremendously comforted. My intuition told me that the memorial service could be helpful to him, and it was. I was so grateful to be able to do something–anything–on this side to help my boy on the other side, and I had.

21 SHORT LIVED

Joshua was our first-born son. He was born in Washington, D.C. on April 12, 1986. To this day, when I see the dogwoods and azaleas in bloom, I think about the day Connie and I brought him home from the hospital to our home in Falls Church, Virginia. Our street was ablaze with springtime color. It seemed like the whole universe was celebrating and heralding the birth of our beautiful baby boy.

I named him Joshua in honor of my two favorite people–Jesus (Jesus is a variation of Joshua; the name means, God is salvation.) and Joshua, the Old Testament leader who led the Israelites out of the wilderness into the Promised Land. I hoped that Joshua would be a blessing to humanity like these men had been.

Joshua's birthday was also a second birthday for me. Before he was born I was just a young man. The day he was born I became something new. I became a father. When I first beheld him, my heart exploded, and a love I didn't know I possessed gushed forth for the first time. I don't know how to explain it, but other fathers may understand. He was so beautiful to me.

He was perfectly formed–his face, his body. He had exquisitely formed hands with long slender fingers. I told Connie, "I think he will have musical ability; he could be a talented pianist." This later turned out to be the case.

He was the easiest baby to care for. He slept through the night from the beginning, and he seldom cried for longer than to tell us he was hungry or needed a new diaper. He was nothing more than a bundle of joy and happiness.

When he was three months old we moved to North Carolina. Within a few years he was joined by three siblings, Gabriel, Ari, and Nadia.

He seemed like a typical youngster, although he showed a delicate, sensitive side. He was full of physical vitality, but I think his social and psychological development lagged a bit.

In retrospect, there were two things that come to mind that might have been warning signs about what was to come. First, although Joshua got along well with his siblings, he sometimes complained about the fact that he had so many brothers and sisters. He could be quite selfish with toys and things. I remember there were a few occasions where he told me, "You and mom had too many kids." We weren't a wealthy family, and I think he figured he would have more of everything if he had been able to remain the center of attention.

Second, on a couple of occasions when he was very young, at maybe two or three, he tried to push my mother-in-law down the half flight of stairs in the entryway of our home. She had moved in with us. He told her she should go away. Again, I think he found her presence in the house a threat to his being the central object of affection. I found his insensitivity disturbing, but chalked it up to his being not much older than a toddler.

Josh kept his feelings inside. He was hard to get really close to for Connie and myself. He wasn't one to easily share his deepest feelings. Nevertheless, I can't say that he was very much different than the average kid.

He did well in elementary school. He was an exceptionally intelligent student, and he was artistically talented as well. The school was small enough that the teachers knew him, the principal knew him, and the environment was safe for his fragile psyche.

Middle school was a disaster.

From the more intimate environment of elementary school, he was thrown into the cauldron of middle school. Instead of having one main teacher, he had a different teacher each period. There were over 1,000 students, so it was impossible for either the teachers or the administrators to get to know their students.

He was bullied and made fun of. The richer kids ridiculed his clothes. I remember he came home one day in tears and said, "Those kids, I hate them! I want to kill them all."

Josh did not possess what the psychologists called coping skills. When he had a problem, he would withdraw, hide from it, and become quietly angry and alienated.

My second son Gabriel was the total opposite. He told Connie and me one day he had been ridiculed in middle school for his clothing. At first it bothered him, but then he developed a coping technique. He would look directly into the eyes of his tormenter and calmly and confidently say, "Look at this face. Does it look like it cares?"

He'd walk away, and the tormenting eventually stopped.

In time, Gabriel went on the offensive. An encounter went something like this:

"So you don't like my shirt? I see you're working for Abercrombie and Fitch," he'd say.

"What do you mean?" responded the tormenter.

"Well, you spent twice as much as I paid for my shirt at Wal-Mart, and now you're walking around advertising for Abercrombie and Fitch. They should be paying you, but you're paying them to give them free advertising."

The contrast between Joshua and Gabriel couldn't have been greater. I used to say to Connie that the assembly line that created the boys got stuck when Josh went through to get his dose of maturity. It skipped over Josh, and then gave Gabriel a double dose.

Even as he struggled, Josh displayed a hilarious sense of humor. He was often side-splittingly funny. He used to do voice impersonations. One of his best was his impression of a guy like Apu, the Kwik-E-Mart clerk in the Simpsons. Once he got that accent going, you would swear the kid had grown up in India. Then there was the time I took him to do a service project in Honduras when he was fifteen. Each group had to do a skit, and he played George W. Bush. His Texas accent and use of the term "Strategery" had me in stitches.

We had gone to Honduras as part of a project of the Religious Youth Service, one of my favorite Unification Church-related charities. Teenagers from all over the world and local Hondurans worked with pickaxes breaking the stony ground to lay a foundation for a cultural center in a small town in the hills outside of Tegucigalpa. It was backbreaking work in the hot near-equatorial sun. I noticed one day that Josh kept working while the other American and European kids had taken a break. Later in the day, I asked him about that.

"Dad," he said with genuine sincerity, "these little Honduran teenagers didn't take a break either. They live off of rice and beans. How could I, a big, strong, well-fed American, take a break? It just didn't seem right." To experience the heart that he had for those less fortunate than he was one of the proudest moments of my life.

We decided to get Josh out of the public school "student warehouse" and into a private Christian school. Connie got a job as a teacher's assistant there to help pay the tuition. We would pay for one child, and the other would be free. So Gabe got to go, too.

The school used the Paideia system of education, which encourages a great deal of interaction between the teacher and the students in the classroom. Teaching is more individualized; the teacher does a lot of coaching and is open to assigning tasks to students based upon their own interests and input. Students are assessed as individuals and not in comparison to the group. Classes are sometimes little seminars, with the students included in group discussion. The boys thrived. They wore uniforms to school, so there were no clothing disputes. They enjoyed studying Latin, sang hymns, and got exposed to a God-centered culture, including prayers.

It was at this time that Josh asked us if we could join a Christian church. "We go to a Christian school," he said. "Shouldn't we be members of a church?"

The boys told me they learned more in that one year than they had in all their public school years combined.

Then the Paideia school fell apart. The founding couple divorced; after the school year ended, every teacher quit except one.

I looked into the possibility of a Catholic School, but the cost was beyond our budget. I struggled with the idea of putting Josh back in a public middle school.

Then his Latin teacher, who was also the principal at the Christian school, told me that Josh was probably intelligent enough to skip the eighth grade and go straight into high school. She was planning to leave the Paideia school to teach Latin at a new charter high school in Raleigh. He might follow her there with several of the other students. She suggested he take the SAT and see if he could score at least 1000, which was a pretty decent score even for a high school kid based on the scoring system that was in place at that time. He surpassed it, even though he was only in the seventh grade.

He started high school the next fall, but he didn't last. As the Latin teacher put it, he had the intelligence, but lacked the emotional maturity.

The only option left was to put him back in a public middle school. We did, but this time it was closer to home, about a mile from our house. We had heard it was a good school.

His life went slowly downhill from there. Josh became more and more distant, secretive, and rebellious. We're pretty sure it was around this time that he began smoking marijuana, although we have no proof.

When he got to high school, he took a strong interest in psychology. From his studies, he was convinced that he had a chemical imbalance in his brain. He diagnosed himself as clinically depressed. He asked if he could see a psychologist in hopes of getting some medication.

I remember that the psychologist was skeptical.

"Our son believes he is suffering from depression," Connie had told him while calling to set the appointment.

"Well," he replied. "It will probably take several sessions before I am able to make that assessment one way or the other."

After only one visit, the psychologist concluded Joshua was indeed depressed and immediately set up an appointment for Josh to see a psychiatrist. The psychiatrist prescribed an antidepressant, Effexor, which seemed to help–at first.

After a few weeks, he stopped taking it. He said his friends told him he "wasn't himself" anymore. He didn't like the way it made him feel, like a zombie, with no feeling inside. We were never able to get him to take it, or any other medication, again.

Josh would sometimes shock us with the things he would say. "I'm not going to live to be 30," he said a couple times. The most disturbing comment was, "I'll probably go out in a blaze of glory."

There was one very bright spot in his last couple of years of life. He met a wonderful girl his sophomore year and fell head-over-heels in love with her. The feeling was mutual. I never saw him as happy as when he was with her. He made a valiant effort to tame his demons and do well in school as well as work part-time after school, largely due to the fact that he wanted to be successful in her eyes. The relationship lasted exactly a year.

After they broke up, Joshua's depression roared back with a vengeance, which is often the case for young men with aching hearts.

***

One morning around 5 am, Connie was awakened by a cry of distress coming from Joshua's bedroom. "Mom...mom...mom" came the troubled plea for help. Opening his door, Connie found him sitting up in bed, his back and head leaning against the wall.

"What's the matter, Joshie?" she asked.

"Mom. I had a bad nightmare." He was breathing heavily and looked terrified.

"There was this searchlight in the sky, moving all around, looking for me. I was trying to escape it, but eventually it found me. When the light hit me, I couldn't move, or talk, or even breathe. It was so scary. Then I woke up."

"Why don't you lay down and I'll rub your back." This was something Connie and I had done for Josh innumerable times before. Often the only way to calm him down and get him to sleep was to rub his back, sometimes for a half an hour or more.

Afterwards, Connie went back to sleep and had a dream with Josh in it. The terrified Josh had transformed into one that was happy and excited. He was giving Connie a tour of his new life.

"Look at my new house," he said, smiling.

He was dressed in his usual black hoodie and pants, but his demeanor was different. He was jovial, kidding around and expressing sincere affection for his mother, which was a rare experience for Connie in those days. He showed her around a house not much different from our own. He seemed proud of his new dwelling, and enjoyed sharing it with his mom.

The scene changed suddenly, and they found themselves inside an ice skating rink. Connie was leaning over the railing watching while Joshua glided over the ice with glee. He was dancing, almost flying, along the ice, smiling broadly in total freedom.

A week later, he was dead.

Joshua's 2nd birthday – I thought he must be the happiest boy in the world.

*Joshua fell asleep while drawing, crayon still clutched in his hand.
I carried this picture with me for years, calling it Artist at Work.*

Happy days! I'm holding my third son Ari. Gabriel is on the left,
Josh is in the middle, and my wife Connie is holding baby Nadia.

Joshua at 15 – in Honduras for a Religious Youth Service project.
Typically, he did something out of the ordinary to his hair.

In hindsight, some pictures strike me as revealing a psyche that wasn't
quite right. Compare this picture of Josh with the
Honduras one and the one on the next page, especially the eyes.

Joshua having a great day at the beach, just a few months before he died.

PART IV THE LETTERS

22 IN MY OWN BACKYARD

After the breakfast session with David was over, Connie and I drove him to the airport to catch his plane back to Seattle, marveling along the way at all that had happened. I felt like I was living in a different dimension, from the intensely spiritual atmosphere in the hospital, the conversation with Josh in his bedroom, the uplifting spirit at his memorial service, and then the profound message from Josh at breakfast. It was all so surreal.

We thanked David for all he had done for us, and then he was off to the West Coast. I couldn't help feeling I would have liked to get on the plane with him. He seemed to have a special connection to the higher realms of reality that I longed for.

On the way back from the airport I thought that if I wanted to have further communication with Joshua I would have to find someone local, but I didn't know where to begin to look.

Someone at the yoga studio knew about a medium in the city of Durham who had successfully removed a ghost from a family member's house.

When I did an Internet search on this medium, I stumbled upon some information that got me very excited–she had been a guest speaker for a large spiritual group in Raleigh.

The name of the group was Spiritual Frontiers Fellowship (SFF), which I immediately recognized from my studies of the afterlife in the 1970s. SFF was founded in the 1950s with the support of one of the most famous mediums of the 20th century, Arthur Ford.

Ford had gained international fame when he contacted the dead son of Bishop James Pike live on network television in 1967.

I was astounded that an active group of SFF had been meeting in Raleigh for over 30 years, right under my nose, and I had never heard about it. This would not be the last time I would be surprised to discover the multitudes of people with various psychic gifts living in my own community. Connie and I immediately made plans to attend their next monthly meeting.

Through SFF, Connie and I did indeed find a local medium, and we were also introduced to the larger community of spiritualists surrounding SFF. This community included a second important organization, the Rhine Research Center and Institute for Parapsychology.

The Rhine Center is headquartered in Durham, about a 30-minute drive from our house. Its founder Dr. J.B. Rhine coined the term Extra Sensory Perception (ESP). We joined a monthly meeting there called the PEG, for Paranormal Experience Group. It was a gathering of individuals, who have had a variety of psychic experiences, who met in a sympathetic environment where they could discuss their experiences without ridicule.

23 RIGHT ON CUE

Through these organizations we were able to meet gifted individuals who provided us with opportunities to communicate with Josh. These encounters are too numerous to go into for the purposes of this book, but there is one in particular that merits mentioning, due to its unexpectedness and the content that was revealed.

The Rhine Center regularly hosts lectures from prominent persons in the field of paranormal phenomena. I didn't attend most of these lectures because they were tailored to scholars and researchers, and I had a hard time relating to them.

One lecture caught my attention though, and Connie and I decided to attend. The topic was psychic detective work, and this was a subject that I found very interesting.

The lecture was presented on a Friday evening, and we arrived at the Rhine Center quite late. As a result, we wound up sitting in the back row. The presenter, a middle-aged woman named Ann, had already concluded her lecture and had begun fielding questions from the audience. I was really disappointed to have missed her speech and chided myself for our tardiness.

My first impression was how typically ordinary Ann was in appearance. She looked like one of the moms you might run into in the stands at a Cary High School football game or the lady in front of you checking out at the grocery store.

Ann held a photograph in her hand and addressed two women in the front row who appeared to be in their forties. The photograph was of a young murder victim who was either a teenager or in his early twenties.

I found her technique intriguing. She would stand there quietly, holding the picture in her hand, looking at it to see what kind of impressions came into her mind.

The two women she spoke to were the victim's mother and his mother's sister.

"When your son was in high school, he was kind of a loner, wasn't he?" Ann asked.

"Yes, that's right. He didn't have many friends," his mother replied.

"And wasn't he a kind of shy, quiet type?"

"Yes," came the response.

The exchange continued like this for a few minutes. Ann would sometimes just stand there quietly for as long as 30 seconds before saying anything. When she spoke, the two women would nod their heads in amazement that this total stranger knew their young family member so well.

This interchange surprised me. I thought that Ann would restrict her talk to her experiences working with the police. It hadn't occurred to me that she might do a little psychic detection live, right on the spot.

"Well," she continued. "I can tell you this much for certain. Your son did not know his attackers. He was a stranger to them. He was murdered through no fault of his own. His is a classic example of the innocent bystander. He was simply in the wrong place at the wrong time."

The exchange continued for a few more minutes, as Ann shared more impressions she received while holding the photograph. Sometimes the women were told things about the young man that even they didn't know, but most of the time they just sat there nodding, confirming Ann's impressions.

There was one exception to her impressions that she got completely wrong, or so we thought.

"What is this about popcorn?" She asked the women.

The mother shook her head, with a puzzled look on her face.

"Did your son have a fondness for popcorn?" she asked.

"Not particularly," she replied. She turned her head to look at her sister, who just shook her head and shrugged.

Ann was silent. After a moment, she spoke again.

"Well, I'm getting this strong impression of popcorn," she said, trying to make sense out of it, and looked at the women again, hoping they could shed some light.

Both of them held up their hands and shook their heads in bewilderment.

Suddenly, I thought I knew what was going on. I raised my hand, hoping Ann could see me in the back row. She did.

"That would be my boy," I said.

"Oh," said Ann, with a little knowing smile on her face.

What had just happened was what I call a cue. Joshua used cues on a few occasions when communicating to us from the other side. To me, a cue is a little piece of information that would be impossible for the medium to know, but lets me know that it's definitely Josh who is communicating. Josh had already used the popcorn cue with a different medium, so I suspected he might be doing it again. Using cues became a favorite way for Josh to make himself known.

Josh used a different cue with a spiritual healer in Raleigh named Mary Mooney. Mary is a Reiki Master with over 20 years of experience practicing the hands-on-healing technique. Once, while participating in a group Reiki session with her, I asked if she could sense Joshua's presence. Mediumship is not central to Mary's work, but she does have the ability to communicate with spirits, among many other gifts.

Mary got quiet for a moment. "Well, there's a young man coming up here, but," and then her voice sounded puzzled, "he's got blue hair!" That was typical Josh. It seemed he changed his hair color with the weather when he was alive on earth. One time it was even bright orange, but I think he really liked it blue. Again, by appearing with blue hair, he was giving a cue to me, because it's something Mary knew nothing about.

One of the most gifted mediums in the United States is a woman that lives in the sunny state of Florida. Joshua used another interesting cue with her. To put it in context–one of my favorite photos of Joshua was taken when he was about three years old. I even gave this photo a title, *Artist at Work*, and carried it around with me for years. In it, Josh is seated at our coffee table drawing large circles in different colors with crayons on white paper. He fell asleep in the chair, still holding a crayon in his hand.

Josh would spend a lot of time drawing with crayons. He would just get so into it that it was hard to get his attention for anything else. When that happened, he just kept going until he fell asleep right in the middle of drawing.

Here's an excerpt from a taped transcript of a telephone reading with Joshua through the mediumship of this woman, October 13, 2007:

Ron Pappalardo:...we need to see if the "popcorn boy" is there and wants to say something.

Medium: Okay, um, there's a little boy here right, uh, coloring. Um, he's busy, he's busy, sitting on the floor. This is a person who passed over but he's showing himself to be about six years old. He's coloring and everybody's calling him to come in the other room for a surprise, and he's busy doing his own thing, but he says he'll be there in a minute.

Uh, wasn't he that way when he was here on the world?

RP: Yes, he was.

Medium: And so, he wants you to know that he's around you.

Josh went on to say that he'd like us to retain the happy memories of his childhood as opposed to his late teens, which were the source of so much turmoil and stress. It was a reassuring message.

Ann finished up with the two women, comforting them and letting them know that she would be working with police investigators to do everything she could to solve the case.

Then she continued taking questions. As the session progressed I began thinking, "Maybe Josh is here, and wants to say something."

I was feeling a bit timid about just jumping up with a question–I didn't want to raise my hand right away because I felt bad about having arrived so late. I decided to wait until all the other people who wanted to ask questions got their chance.

I was grateful that after the last person asked a question, Ann was still willing to take another, so I raised my hand.

I only said one thing, being careful not to reveal any information at all.

"Let's see if the 'popcorn boy' has something to say."

"Okay," Ann said.

I stood up and, reaching into my back pocket, I pulled out my wallet. Inside, I carried pictures of Connie and the kids. I took out a photo of Josh, a copy of his high school portrait, walked up to the front of the room, and handed it to Ann without speaking a word.

Before I returned to my seat, she began to speak.

"Is this your son?" she asked.

"Yes," I replied.

Then she paused for a moment as I sat down. "Is he a suicide?"

The look on Connie's face was one of shocked amazement.

"Yes," I confirmed.

Then she mentioned a few things about Josh's personality and what he was like at high school, all of which seemed accurate.

"Your son had been struggling with his mind for a long time," she said. Then she asked, "What is this about water?"

I didn't know what she was referring to.

"I'm getting some water, maybe a lake? And there's some type of boat, or a canoe."

I was confused. I looked at Connie, who looked just as puzzled. A few moments of silence passed, and then it dawned on me–Pisgah.

"Well, I don't know about a lake," I said, "but we did go whitewater rafting on the Nantahala River one time."

"Oh, Okay," she said.

"He got bumped out of the raft in the rapids, and if I hadn't pulled him back in, he might have drowned," I explained.

"Right. Well, he just wants you to know, that at the time, he was really angry at you for doing that," she said matter-of-factly.

I was stunned, but it all made sense. I understood now why he had made no effort to get back in the raft. Josh had been only 13 at the time, but he was already trying to find a way to get to the other side.

24 VOICE FROM THE PAST

Imagine how it could change your life if you could get a "letter" from your closest loved one who had passed into the spirit world. Something like that happened to me in September 2003; a most profound communication came to us from out of the blue, from a totally unexpected source. To explain it requires a little background.

A couple of months before Joshua crossed over, another young man had gone to the spirit world before him. His name was Homer Boutte. He was 21, and lived in a rural area in upstate New York. He loved the outdoors, and one day while climbing a waterfall, he fell to his death. The death was ruled as an accident by the authorities. His parents were old acquaintances from our days in the Unification Church, but I hadn't spoken to either one of them for at least 10 years.

Meanwhile, living in a different part of the country was another old friend from our church days. We lived in the same community in the 1980s in the Washington, D.C. area. Ironically, she brought a gift for Joshua at his baby shower in 1986. Like the Bouttes, we hadn't spoken to her for many years.

Because this woman wishes to remain anonymous, I will refer to her simply as Ms. Haversham. She was well known in our circle as a person with healing abilities.

I didn't know that Ms. Haversham also has the gift of a type of automatic writing. Simply put, automatic handwriting is a form of mediumship in which a spirit temporarily uses the brain of a medium to transmit a message in the form of written words. The impressions come into the brain of the medium, and he or she writes them down, or, as in Ms. Haversham's case, types them into a computer.

Ms. Haversham learned about Homer's death and out of sympathy for the Bouttes, offered to do an automatic handwriting session with him. After receiving their second letter from Homer through Ms. Haversham, Alice Boutte called Connie and me about a month after Josh's passing.

"Hello, Ron and Connie, this is Alice Boutte," came the familiar voice from New York.

"Hello, Alice. Wow, it's been a long time since we've talked, hasn't it?" I said.

"Yeah," she said. "Time sure flies. Look, I'm so sorry to hear about Josh."

"Thank you, Alice," I said. "It means so much to us that you took the time to call."

"Yeah, I know," she said, with a familiar sadness in her voice.

Then Alice broke the news to me of her son's passing, of which I had been unaware, and told me about Ms. Haversham.

"I had no idea she had mediumship abilities," I said.

"Yeah, well, she doesn't like to advertise it, so I'm not surprised. We've received two letters from Homer through Ms. Haversham, and he mentions meeting your son in the spirit world in the latest one."

"What?" I exclaimed. "You've got to be kidding me."

"No, really," she replied. "You want me to read it to you?"

"Sure," I said, excitedly.

"Hold on a minute and let me see if I can find it," she said, setting the phone down. A minute later she was back.

"Here it is," she said. "It's quite long, so I'm just going to read part of it. I can send the whole thing to you if you like."

"Sure, please do," I said.

"Okay, Homer says, 'I am also often with other Second Generation kids, like Andrew. Also, there are other kids. Recently we helped, together, to welcome and guide along another young man–Josh Pappalardo. He is still sleeping a lot, but we were there to greet him and we have visited with him. His passing was turbulent but he is resting quietly now.'

"Ron, the Andrew he mentions is Andrew Byrne," Alice said. "You know his parents. Andrew died in a car accident a while back."

The letter was dated August 21, 2003, so it was received only 10 days after Josh's passing, and a little over two months since Homer's passing on June, 11, 2003. This was all so amazing to me, and it also added more pieces to the puzzle to complete the picture of what happened. "Second Generation" is a term Unificationists use to describe children of the original church members, which would include my kids, too. It's my guess that these children were the "beings of light" that approached Joshua after he crossed over and who tried to get him to go with them into the spirit world. Like he said in his bedroom, "they're good, but I don't know any of these people."

The connection came through the parents. We all knew each other, and there was a deep bond of the heart connecting all of us. Somehow this connection affected the children as well.

I never met any of these kids either, but I know Alice Boutte to be one of the kindest and gentlest souls I have ever known. I remember Andrew's father, Shawn, very well and was saddened by his fairly recent passing. Shawn Byrne had been a Catholic priest from Ireland before he became involved with the Unification Church, and I felt an immediate connection to him, having been raised Catholic myself, under the care of Irish priests.

"Ron, I'm sure Ms. Haversham would want to do a reading for the two of you with Josh," Alice said. "You should call her. Do you have her number?"

"No," I said.

Alice found the number for us and I called Ms. Haversham as soon as we finished our conversation.

25 BIRDS OF A FEATHER

There was another connection between Joshua and Homer that I was not aware of. This connection was confirmed in the last of three letters from Homer to his parents, received through Ms. Haversham on June 4, 2004, a portion of which is reproduced here:

I was here with Josh Pappalardo a few days ago, and I know he is doing so well. He is a totally different person than when he came here.

In the spirit world it is as if we shed this shell that we thought was us, and the real person shines through. It's a person we knew in our hearts, the person we felt was us but that we could never quite connect with consciously. At least that was the case with me in the physical world. I always think about Mrs. Jones because she tried so hard to reach that person in me and draw it out. She'd say something like, "Yeah, that's it" as if to encourage "Homer" to come out of his shell. But then I would babble on and totally lose touch with it. I was so frustrated.

Mom, it was as if some special connectors were missing in my brain that I could never find. In a sense, this was a source of bliss in my younger years. And so I was a happy child even though things around me may have been tense or problematic. But as I grew into adulthood, I could not handle the world. It was as if a filter was missing, and I could not find it. So I was bombarded with notes that did not harmonize into music that did not make sense. It was other people's stuff mixed with mine and, I could not distinguish the "me" from my environment. I just became a jumble of stuff, bits of this and that.

Of course, at the time, I was overwhelmed with fear. Terror is more like it. I had waves of terror. I saw no hope at times. Then I would encounter periods of total clearness, and I was fine.

...In a way, I had to forget a lot of what happened in my life—especially more recently to my passing. That was sort of my healing. Then I could gather my energies and begin to re-construct myself as "Homer" as a child. From here I grew quickly to become a young adult and to move into my space of wholeness. This process took months of

physical time. But for me it was very quick. I went through intervals of sleep. I was visited by beings of light and love who imparted healing to me. And I went through such periods of total peace that words cannot describe this.

And so, with time I could face myself and forgive me. It was never my intention to take my life. Whereas others in my shoes, with my disability I will call it, would have pondered suicide and perhaps attempted it, I never allowed myself into this space. This is just not an option that I ever sought.

Although Homer's death had been ruled an accident, not suicide, I could still see a connection in the mindset that both boys shared. Both boys were very happy as young children, and both began to feel more and more out of place and disoriented as they grew older. In Joshua's case, this process began with the arrival of adolescence; in Homer's, it started with the onset of adulthood. Both felt out of place in the world, and both felt that some vital connections in their brain functions were missing. Knowing there were some similarities in their inner states of mind, it makes more sense to me that Homer would establish a close relationship with my son when Joshua arrived on the other side. As I pondered Homer's situation, being pried away from life in the midst of the beauty of nature, my mind returned again to the swirling rapids of the Nantahala River, and the strangely serene look on Joshua's face as the waters pulled him away.

This passage also reinforces a key reason why I encourage people in these situations to seek spirit communication, particularly in cases of suicide or other types of traumatic death. The emotional turmoil that can result on both sides of life can be healed in this way. Both the victim and the ones left behind can benefit from the communication.

One can understand, from the closing passage of Homer's letter to his parent's received on August 21, 2003, how comforting this communication can be:

"I want to convey to all of you that I love you very much. I am with you and I appreciate your love and support for me. When you remember me, instead of becoming overwhelmed by our separation, be grateful for the life we spent together, the love we shared, and the experiences we had – no matter how mundane. This is what I am trying to do as well. A big hug and kisses for everyone.

"Love. Homer"

The spirit world is not a world of gross matter. It is a world that is more affected by thought and emotion than by material things. So, it is often important that spirits have the opportunity to sort out their thoughts and feelings by working them out with loved ones or others on the earth. For this, spirit communication is very beneficial.

26 LIBERATION

A few days elapsed between the time we talked to Ms. Haversham about performing a reading with Josh and the reading itself.

The phone rang on September 24, 2003. It had been about six weeks since Josh's passing.

"I made contact with Josh," Ms. Haversham said. "It was very emotional. I went through a whole box of tissues. Usually, these readings take about 40 minutes, but this one was over 2 hours. He had a lot he needed to say, and there was a lot of crying along the way. I'm going to send this out to you right away."

When the letter arrived, I would not look at it at first. Connie read it before I did, and was very comforted by it. Intuitively, I knew that reading that letter would be like opening the cork on a bottle of champagne that had been shaken vigorously. I knew a lot of bottled up emotions were going to explode out of me, and I was pretty sure it would be a messy ordeal.

I waited for a time when Connie and the kids had left the house. I knew they were going to be gone for a while. I locked the doors, turned off the ringers on the phones, and went upstairs, locking the door to my bedroom behind me. I was honestly embarrassed at what might happen when I read the letter.

I began to pray. I prayed in a very simple, childlike manner, talking to my heavenly Father as a little boy would talk to his dad. No pretension. Total honesty and sincerity. I told God what I had been going through and how I felt. I asked him to read the letter together with me; we would face this thing together.

I've reproduced the entire contents of the letter here exactly as it was given to me; I haven't added a single word, nor removed any.

Do I really believe this came from my son? It sure sounds like him! Even the style of speech. Also, there is information included that Ms. Haversham couldn't possibly have known about. I won't know for sure until

I cross over, but I'd be willing to bet the deed to my house that it came from him.

The words in parentheses are comments Ms. Haversham makes while she received the dictation.

The letter opens with greetings from a group of spirits who helped to provide the energy for the communication to take place. Think of them as a big spiritual "radio transmitter."

Reading with Josh Pappalardo, September 24, 2003:

This is the Council of Light. We want to express to the parents of Josh that we are just beings of heart who wish to create a bridge that can allow loved ones to communicate freely and casually between these worlds, the physical and the spiritual. So we are here at your calling on their behalf as they seek communication with Josh.

Josh is here and we are with him now. He is a bright young man, bright as his parents truly know him to be, but not as he appeared in recent times leading to his passing. For this he has much regret. Not only that he was in a slump (as he calls it) for so long, but that they cannot see how truly bright he is now. We will let him speak as he is very able to communicate, and he is anxious to express himself to his family.

Mom, Dad, this is Josh. I am speaking with my heart, and I am so relieved that you can receive my words as if I am speaking them directly to you. I feel so much love and light and energy coming from you, and this totally is changing me. Well, it is not changing me so much as it is freeing me to be myself.

I want to begin by saying how sorry I am for putting you through this horrible, senseless experience. For me, it was "another day in the messed up life of Josh," but I know that for you it was a real shock, and I can see that it has caused you so much pain. This burdens me, and I sincerely apologize. Please forgive me, and please forgive yourselves also because you really are not at fault. I made choices that were bad choices. That is the amazing thing about growing up. We reach a point in our lives where we can make choices, and we sometimes just make stupid ones that lead into more stupid ones, and it's all a downward spiral. Of course, I didn't see this when I was on the earth. I was just caught up in the emotions and the energy of rebellion. It was an addiction to rebellion. It gave me a sense of control and escape at the same time. What I didn't realize is that it was propelling me into oblivion! And so this is where it brought me.

I wish that I could say that everything is all right and I am happy, but you know that I am not. Just as you are suffering, I am too. I have to face what I have done, which is a big violation of the gift of life, and it is a slap in the face of those who created me. I was born of love—yours, God's, the whole universe's. And I snuffed out my life on earth in a moment of thoughtlessness. This is hard to reconcile, and it causes me great pain. I also disrupted the lives of my younger siblings in ways that are difficult for anyone to comprehend, and I regret this deeply. I ask also for their forgiveness. Please, please know that I love you deeply and I am crazy about you. You mean all the world to me, and I would never have imagined that I could hurt you so by doing this before your eyes. Please forgive me, and please choose a good experience we had together and record this as the memory you had of us together, not those last months and hours I had on the earth. This will free my heart and allow me to feel your mercy. I need that from you so much.

So this is what weighs so heavily in my heart—the family and friends whom I hurt through my stupid choices, my attitude, and my passing. I took my life, and no one should feel so proud before God and their parents as to feel that they have the right to do this. Mom and Dad, please don't try to just skim over these words from my heart because they may bring you pain and regret. I need to express this from my heart because it is what I am working through at this time. It is a road I must travel in the process of healing. I want to walk it with you. Please, please hear me. I love you so much, and I need you to feel this love because I know that in the last years and months I have not expressed it to you. In my rebellion I tried to hurt the world back, and it was you who I was hurting. It was you, and I am so shocked to see what I was doing to you. How could I have been so blind in my heart not to see this?

(He cries at this point and is silent)

Dad, I am so proud of you as my father. I am so proud to be your son.

(He cries again)

The dark energy that I created through rebellion and attitude became darker and more powerful than me, it engulfed me. My soul was lost in this dark cloud of energy. It was like a tornado. I could not think, feel or move inside anymore. I just got swept up in the power, the roar and confusion of the twister—and I was gone. I also turned everyone else's lives upside down. You were left to pick up the pieces after the storm.

I was dead a long time before I took my life. I died inside. It was like an implosion. I have to say that by the time I took my life I had no feeling of myself left to get in touch with, much less those around me. This is why I could do such a terrible thing. I just didn't feel anymore. I didn't start out this way. Please understand this, because I am just slowly piecing this together. I just started out trying to express myself and to create my identity separate from what I thought was false and wrong (with religion, society, the established traditions). But in the process, I fueled my ideas with other energies. I eventually could not separate myself from those energies, and I was changing so fast, even for myself.

Dad, can you do this for me? Can you please share this with my friends? I am not the only one in this space. Some of my friends are also caught up in this energy. Don't label it as "evil sources" because it turns people off. Just say it in my words.

It is energy we generate with our thoughts, attitudes, the things we read, listen to, and see that reinforces our negative thinking. Tell them to step back and breathe, be quiet with themselves and listen to their hearts. Tell them to not lose touch with their souls, who they truly are within. I was so surprised Dad to find that my soul was so bright deep inside. I could not believe this was me. I scarcely had a feel for myself in the end, and when I could, I only saw darkness. But that wasn't me. And the world around me was not all that bad. It was ME who was seeing only the bad. We create the reality around us. Please just share this with my friends, even if just one or two want to hear me out, please let them know that this is what happened to me. It does not have to happen to them. Not that anyone will be so stupid as to take their life. I know this took a lot of courage for me—stupid courage, but they don't need to live in such darkness. It is not necessary. Dad, don't be concerned about whether they accept this or not, just share it with them and anyone who may be struggling in a similar situation as myself. It is the truth, and it will speak to them deeply in their hearts if they are ready to hear it. I am close to my friends, and will try to convey this to them in other ways as well. It's just that it's so amazing to me that I can express it in words through this communication.

Mom, I love you, and I will always remember your love and your words of comfort as you tried to understand me, to reach me. We are still in touch with each other. Know this, that I am more present in your lives now than I have been in several years even though I was on the earth then. And I can talk to you directly, even without Ms. Smith.

I am getting the support I need here to grow and to rise above the issues that I have carried with me. It's all love here, no judgment. I am surrounded by very loving beings who tend to my needs and encourage me to venture outside of my shell that I had created for myself.

I want to tell you that I have met a young man named Andrew Byrne. He is such a good person, and he approaches me as if we have known each other forever. He puts his arm around me, and he shows me that he cares. He is so bright, and he also told me about his life and some of his mistakes. He says that he also had issues when he passed. He didn't take his life like me. He was careless (that means wild) he says, and he found himself here in a flash. He has helped me through this period of regret. It is so hard to rise above regret. But he is here with me often, and I am so grateful to him. Others come who passed in the same manner as I–by taking their own lives. Everyone's story is different, yet so similar. And no one judges me. They just bring love and encouragement. So you should know that who I'm hanging out with on this side you would very much approve of. (He laughs)

I leave you now. My love to everyone and especially to my siblings. I appreciate everyone's prayers and light and love. This all gets translated into wonderful support in the form of uplifting thoughts and feelings that last. This is what sustains me–your love.

I wave good-bye to you. I feel I never said good-bye. This talk has lifted a heavy burden from my heart. I know that I was emotional and maybe heavy at times, but know that this has been very good for me–to express what was deep in my heart freely to you, and to know that you receive it with love. I also felt restless because I naturally wanted to communicate this message to my friends. I know that you will help me do this Dad. You always respected me. I know that you think you were probably not caring enough. But you just were upset at that "monster" that had become me, and very rightfully so. You were upset at me for allowing myself to let this monster of energy consume me. I understand this now.

Bye. Love. Josh.

Tears began to well up in my eyes immediately as I began to read the letter. It was strange. It sounded just like Josh, but it sounded like a Josh from years back. It didn't sound like the Josh of the recent past. It was as if a demon had been exorcised from him, and he sounded more like the young son with whom I had shared a closer connection than the troubled rebel of his adolescence. I felt like I got my son back, but this made all the more raw the feeling of intense longing I had for his physical presence. I missed him terribly. I wanted to be able to give him a hug–to hold him close–but I could not. I wanted to see him face to face.

I was holding up fairly well emotionally until I got to the part where Ms. Smith said he paused and began to cry, and then he said the words my soul had been aching to hear:

Dad, I am so proud of you as my father. I am so proud to be your son.

Immediately upon hearing these words, the dam that was holding in my emotions burst asunder. I wailed loudly as the feelings poured out from deep within my soul. Tears rolled down my cheeks and my nose ran and ran. Saliva even oozed from my mouth. I became a soggy mass of wet. Meanwhile, my stomach churned inside my gut, the muscles becoming sore from the intense contractions. The noise of my wailing would probably have been disturbing to anyone who heard it. I grabbed a pillow and buried my face in it to mask the sound–my wailing was so loud I thought someone might call the police.

The agony of the years of stress and anxiety over the struggle to save my boy gushed out the way water flows from an open fire hydrant.

The spectacle of a grown man in the depths of grief is an awesome sight. I've seen pictures from Iraq of masculine, middle-aged men grieving over dead sons–eyes bloodshot, faces twisted in anguish, liquid oozing from every orifice. This is what I must have looked like. It had been over a month since Joshua had passed, yet I was only now allowing myself the luxury of letting it all out, and even though it hurt, it hurt in a good way.

Within the cascade of jumbled emotions, two stood out above the rest. They emerged like two mighty stones protruding from the middle of a swirling whirlpool, offering me refuge from the flood–forgiveness and liberation.

I hadn't been able to escape the thought that maybe his death had all been my fault, that if I had somehow done something differently, Josh would still be with us. I thought Josh might be blaming me from the other side, caught up in bitter anger at the father who failed him. I was concerned that if he harbored such resentment, it would be a shackle for him. Now I knew that he was not bound by such chains. He was free, and because he was free, I was also free. I felt the joy of liberation beginning to soothe my soul.

If he could say, "I'm proud to be your son" it meant that, from the other side, he now understood what I had gone through. He knew now the efforts and sacrifices that both Connie and I had made to try and help him. He saw the sleepless nights, the prayers, and the frustration at not being able to reach him.

Along with liberation I felt forgiveness. I could start to forgive myself, and I knew that Joshua had forgiven me as well. In the days and weeks that followed, I would start to love myself again.

After several minutes, I slowly began to calm down. The reservoir of grief poured itself out and began to taper off, quietly ebbing away. In a few more minutes it was all over, and it felt as if I had arrived at the beginning point of my healing.

27 HOPE

As a result of the letter, I felt sure that Josh was going to be all right. Even though I felt so much liberation and hope from his letter, it didn't diminish the fact that I missed him like crazy.

One day, Connie and I saw a boy about Josh's age walking through the parking lot of a shopping center near our home. He not only looked like Josh, he walked and dressed like him, too. Both of us stopped dead in our tracks and just watched him walk along through the parking lot, just looking at the back of him until he was finally out of sight. Anyone who saw us would have wondered if we were crazy. Just watching this boy walk by was such a joy. It brought back the old familiar feeling I used to get gazing at my son, delighting in his existence.

One of the hardest things for me to come to terms with was the fact that I would never get the chance to see Joshua's children. There would be no grandchildren from his lineage. No Joshua Junior to play with or take fishing. This realization filled me with sorrow.

Though I missed him so much, I knew that Josh was learning a lot in his new environment. To handle the terrible longing we had to see him, I told Connie, "If it helps you, just pretend he's away at college. That's what I do." So I kind of tricked my mind into believing he was just away at school, and I comforted myself by knowing that if I couldn't stand the separation anymore, we could always try to get another letter from him if we needed it.

The separation was becoming unbearable when we asked Ms. Haversham for a second letter a couple of months later. It arrived in December. This one revealed that Joshua was making exceptional progress, and was even more comforting than the first one:

December 6, 2003:

Hi, this is Josh. Thanks for seeking me out today, Ms. Haversham. And thanks also for taking the time to open this communication for the sake of my parents. I have been waiting at your door for some time, and I hope you are not mad at me, but I knew you would try to reach me, and I wanted to be ready. I know how busy you are, so I appreciate this.

Hi Mom and Dad. Hi to everyone! I know you think that I am somewhere far away, but you would be so amazed to discover that I am right here with you. There is not like distance between us in space, but distance in consciousness. In other words, the distance is really in our minds. Isn't it that way with so many things–just distortions of the mind! So much has happened since I last sent my communication to you. For me here, everyday is a day of new discoveries. I am willing to change, so just to have that willingness affords me many opportunities for growth and new experiences. Not that it is easy. I am challenged in so many ways. If I have a gripe toward my parents for how you raised me as your son it is that you made life too easy for me. This may be a shock to my younger brothers and sister, but it is the truth. I realize that I was very sheltered in my life and I knew nothing of what it was to do without and to suffer and to give. Here, we grow only by giving of ourselves, by putting ourselves out there for others. It is the same on the earth, but we just don't understand it as this. We think on the earth that intellect and money and position in society are what give us value. But that is not true. It just is the furthest thing from the truth. I am not saying that everyone thinks this way, or that this is how you taught me. All I am saying is that is what I thought and believed. And this is how most people I encountered lived.

Here, we are stripped down to our soul, and nothing outside of this has much bearing on who we are or what we do. And so, I discovered that I am just a child. Mom and Dad, I was just a child. I thought I was all grown up, but I was just a little boy, acting out in the body of a young adult. Coming to this awareness was very sobering to me. If you need me to translate this into earth years so you have an idea how young I was emotionally and spiritually, I would say I was about 6 or 8 years. Now, I can see my Dad nodding and going "No wonder!" (He chuckles here).

So this is how I started my life on this side, so young. You will be very happy to know that I am growing fast here. I have no idea how old I would now be in earth years, but I am no longer hanging out with the "kiddies" around here. That should give you some hope. (He chuckles again). We don't go by calendars and clocks around here and we don't have physical form that shows age. We just are.

In talking with my friends here who came to this side in the same manner as myself, we all agree that were we mature to the level where we are now in our age, we would never have made this decision to take our lives as we did. And so our conclusion is that we are just not educated properly on the earth about what really matters in life–which is our emotional and spiritual development. If half the energy were devoted to this that is now devoted to the concerns of where we stand in society and who we are and what people think of us, we would soon outgrow all these stupid concerns because we would just "grow up!" I know I was a kid when I passed to this side, but at least I was still just a young person. Many people come here as full-grown adults, and they are just kids as well. Imagine their shock.

These are just my observations. You know me, always thinking these things through and trying to make sense of everything. I just can't let go of something until I figure it out and it seems right and just. These were sources of great frustration for me on the earth. I just could not understand so many things. I couldn't put two and two together, and I became disillusioned with life and with people, even with my parents, whom I looked up to and loved deeply. Now you can understand that I was just a little boy trying to understand this stuff. I was trying to put a puzzle together, but I did not have all the pieces of the puzzle, nor did I have a clear image of the puzzle itself. I often felt that somehow things that seemed to be so important to me didn't seem so relevant to others around me. This frustrated me deeply, and it made me irritated and angry. I am saying this in the first tense now, but it seems as if I am talking about another person. I have changed so much.

Ms. Haversham is eating popcorn as she takes this dictation, and this amuses me. It's okay with me. I think it helps her keep going, but what she doesn't realize is that I was having a desire for popcorn, and she just walked over and she just got into it! (He chuckles, and I realize that I never eat when I take dictation, but I did this so naturally, and then have consumed a whole bowl of it in a flash!)

And so my life on this side is all right. I am at peace. I am not so anxious and hyper as when I last spoke to you. I actually feel more settled, and I am gaining a better sense of myself and my surroundings. I also have freedom to move out of this area where I live. Many who pass to this side turn right around and start helping others. I am not there yet. I am still being cared for and taught, because you know, I was just a boy. Andrew visits me often and I have made many new friends here.

And talking about friends, Dad, thanks for sharing my words with my friends. I am taking care of them. In a way, I also feel responsible because I had very weird ideas, and I think that I may have poisoned the minds of some of my friends by sharing my stupid thoughts. So I was so glad when you could share "my reflections from the other side" (he chuckles) with them. I also feel responsible for some of the issues of my younger siblings because I think that I may have contributed to their problems. Dad and Mom, please know that I am taking care of my younger brothers and sister. I am being a good older brother to them, and you will see that it makes a difference in their lives in the long run. Don't make their lives difficult just because I said you were too easy on me. That was just me. You would really ruin my relationship with them. (And he chuckles again)

Mom, I know that with time you will become so aware of how close I am with you that you will not miss me anymore. This is a good way to grow and develop the gift of moving in and out of the two worlds—the physical and spiritual, because I am on this side and we can communicate. I am doing very well. Maybe it helps you to pretend that I am away at school (which is sort of true) and we will see each other again soon (which is true). The heart is very amazing. You can play tricks on it like this and it works. Try it.

I give my love to everyone, and now that Christmas is coming I want to tell you that I will visit you and share this season with you as a shining bright star. You will know it is me when I visit you in this time. Let's have a happy Christmas. Please don't be sad. I feel so responsible for making your lives so difficult in the last few months since I made the decision to take my life. We all (who have done this) search in vain for ways to heal the wounds we cause to our families when we take our own lives in this way.

I love you all very much.

Josh

Note from Ms. Haversham: Josh was very candid and light-hearted. He seems so much in control of his life and he appears to be very self-satisfied. A lot of it may come from his coming to finally understand issues that he couldn't figure out on earth (as he expresses). It was a real joy to do this reading with him, so different from the last time, which was all tears.

Indeed, what a joy it was to get this letter! Josh sounded so happy.

From another perspective, Connie and I found it so amazing that we had been just recently talking about pretending Josh was away at college. Josh affirmed this at the end of the letter where he says:

Maybe it helps you to pretend that I am away at school (which is sort of true) ... The heart is very amazing. You can play tricks on it like this and it works.

Then there is the use of the popcorn cue again, with a little twist. Josh was actually able to influence Ms. Haversham to make some popcorn, and he received vicarious pleasure from her eating it. She told us over the phone how surprised she was that he got her to do this; he always did have a mischievous streak.

Finally, I had taken Josh's request from his first letter seriously, and made copies of the letter for distribution to his friends. He acknowledged this in the second letter as well:

And talking about friends, Dad thanks for sharing my words with my friends.

Ms. Haversham had no idea about the pretending, the popcorn, or the friends. Was it just three lucky guesses? As I said before, I can't prove these words are from Joshua, but the evidence is pretty persuasive.

28 WHAT LIFE IS LIKE IN "HEAVEN"

I have already written of my struggle to reconcile the traditional Christian view of suicide with what I felt to be true in my heart. Obviously, the doctrine of damnation to eternal Hell-fire was contradicted by the communications we received from Joshua.

These communications open up larger questions regarding historically accepted views about the purpose of life and the nature of each soul's inevitable transition to the spirit world after the event called "death."

As a result of my Roman Catholic education as a child, I had come to believe that life was a sort of testing ground or contest of the soul, in which one spends his or her life in a constant battle to maintain vigilance against the inclination we humans seem to possess to commit sin and evil; at the end of this contest, we die and confront our Judgment Day. We are sentenced to either Heaven or Hell, and the judgment is final.

Joshua's experience, however, is quite different, and not so dogmatic. Speaking about those who hold these views and then cross over to the spirit world he says:

"They get to death and then everything is 'the end.' There is no room in their minds to conceive of what is beyond physical existence, even if they believe in life after death, and so the word that is used is 'death,' the end, finished. But there is so much more! ...

"I think that we all believe that we accomplish what we came to the earth to accomplish in our lifetime. But that is not necessarily the case. We continue to grow in spirit." 1/11/2009

So death is not the end of our growth, and if it is possible to grow in the spirit world, then even if there is what we might call a Hell, it cannot be eternal. There must be a way out even for the most hopeless soul. It appears that the soul must, however, possess or develop an openness and willingness to change and grow; we have seen that there are innumerable spirits on the other side that are eager to assist anyone who desires to make that effort:

"I was so blessed to have made a very quick transition and to have moved into a higher consciousness. And so, I could leave the old concepts of what is life behind and embrace the world of Being, just being one with God, the universe, everyone and everything that is alive. But many young people that I work with are stuck in the past. They cannot forgive and so they re-live the past over and over. We try to reach them in many ways and we never give up. I love them so much Mom. Can you believe it, I love? And it is this love that eventually draws them out of their pain." 5/29/05

There are many other traditional religious concepts about life after death that I have had to modify or abandon altogether as a result of Joshua's communications as well as the communications of others from the spirit world. They are too numerous to explore fully for the purposes of this book, but I think it is important, as well as fascinating, to touch on a few of them here.

When Joshua was alive on the earth, like many teenagers, he was crazy about video games and other similar diversions. After entering the spirit world, the obsession with being entertained gradually diminished:

"We don't have video games, TV, Nintendo and things like that here. Anyway, that is so superficial to what is real and alive here that we never desire it. Well, I did when I first came to this side and was still tied to the physical realm with my thoughts and emotions. But having moved to other realms of light totally frees us of the strings that tie us to stuff of the world." 5/30/2004

That's not to say that life in the spirit world is boring. Far from it! Joshua describes with great enthusiasm diversions, if you can call them that, which are a lot more exciting than playing a video game:

"Life is so rich and bright and beautiful here. I have flown. I have flown and it is so amazing. We fly like birds here. No airplanes, no ultra lites, just our arms outstretched, and free as birds!" 5/30/2004

Musical and artistic activities make up an important part of life in the spirit world. There are areas in the spirit world devoted to these pursuits.

As the spirit makes progress in the spiritual world, it appears that the emphasis on the individual self or ego that seems to be so central to our modern Western way of thinking diminishes over time:

"Transitioning to the spiritual world affords us the opportunity to blend back into the source of all that is, to lose ourselves and the particular identities we took on while on the earth and become one with

the Source. We move from this tiny sense of insignificant self, to a feeling of wholeness and completeness that is difficult to describe. We are one heartbeat, one breath, one essence together with all that is—the wind, music, others...spirit.

"My parents like to look at photos of me as a child and remember what life was like with me. The truth is that what they are trying to grasp is the 'feeling' of Josh, and that feeling of Josh is in them because I am in them. You look puzzled Ms. Haversham. I know it's hard to conceive of what I am trying to convey, but just say it this way. My Mom is an artist. They get it.

"And so, that self-absorption that one finds so difficult to shake even upon transitioning to this side, is gone. My sense of Josh as I lived on the earth is faded and all I know is that I am a part of my parents' lives, my family and friends. I matter to them and they matter to me. I impacted the lives of others—in good ways and I am proud of that. I have let go of that which was painful and difficult to comprehend about my life existence, so I cannot tell you much of that. It is not in my space."
1/11/2009

Even though the spirit person experiences this profound oneness with Divinity and with others as well, it is my sense that the individual personality is not lost. It is just that there is a much stronger feeling of connectedness. My son still exhibits from time to time the same outrageously funny sense of humor and even that certain mischievousness he has always had. In that sense, he is the same Josh I knew on earth, the same unique and irreplaceable personality. What has changed is a profound growth in his sensitivity to the feelings of others, and a pronounced awareness of how connected he is to everyone. As a parent, it's a very rewarding and awesome thing to observe.

It is my view that the individual personality will always survive, and I have a theory as to why that is the case. It is all about the importance of relationships. No one likes to be alone. I don't think even God wants to be alone. Everyone wants to have someone else to relate to, and to love.

It is often said that "God is love," and yet, it is essential to remember that love can only be realized or fulfilled when there is a relationship with someone other than yourself. It takes two, not one. So even though we will, I believe, eventually all experience directly Divine Union in the love embrace of our Creator, it will be clear to us that we are not ourselves God, but God's beloved partner in love. We will experience oneness with the Divine, while retaining our own unique personalities.

Regarding the question of spiritual growth, it appears that there are progressive levels of growth to be attained in the spirit world. Happily, this view seems to be in accordance with many faith traditions here on earth. Most of us are familiar with Jesus' remark that "In my Father's house are many mansions..." (John 14:2 KJV). The apostle Paul also refers to different levels in the spirit world:

"I know a person in Christ who fourteen years ago was caught up to the third heaven – whether in the body or out of the body I do not know; God knows." (2 Cor. 12:2 NRSV)

A spirit can travel to a higher level in one of two ways; one can either attain the level of spiritual growth required to dwell in a higher place, or one can temporarily visit a higher realm in the company of a higher spirit who acts as a sort of escort and guide.

Each successive level exists at a different vibration than the previous one, and if the spirit person is unable to "breathe" the atmosphere in the higher realm, he or she will find it difficult to stay for any prolonged period of time. What is the atmosphere made of in the spirit world? Apparently, one is "breathing" the actual love of God.

A good analogy is mountain climbing. In order to climb a mountain, a person must train. Most important are the lungs. If the lungs do not have the capacity to breathe the air as it becomes more rarefied at the higher elevations, the climber will have to descend or make use of some equipment, such as oxygen tanks, to continue ascending.

Higher spirits have the ability to surround others with extra energy, like the oxygen tank provides more oxygen, to allow the lesser developed spirit to visit the higher realm. Spirits who visit these levels return with awe-inspiring stories of the brightness and beauty of these realms, as well as the extraordinary levels of heart and love possessed by the spirits who dwell there. I suspect that part of the reason for these journeys to the higher realms is to inspire and encourage others to work to attain the ability to visit them on their own merit and power.

One doesn't have to die in order to visit the spirit world, as a temporary visitor, of course. There are many accounts of people throughout history who have had such experiences.

A famous example is the story of Fatima, Portugal, where in 1917 a spirit identifying herself as Mary, the Mother of Jesus, appeared to three children in a series of visions. In one of these encounters, Mary allowed the children to see into the lower realms of the spirit world, where they observed great suffering. Interestingly, Mary told the children that many souls go to hell because they have no one to pray or make sacrifices for them, which seems to confirm my conviction that there is a way for even the darkest of souls to rise into higher realms, contradicting the traditional doctrine of eternal and immutable damnation. It also supports Joshua's message that the love and prayers we project on his behalf have a powerful positive effect on him in the spirit world.

Joshua encourages me to try to open my spiritual senses so that I can experience his realm directly. He once said he'd like to grab me by the arm and bring me up for a "look-see":

"If you could see the brilliance of this world that I live in, experience the wholeness that is, you would be so comforted and you would be so happy, not just because you would know that I am fine, but because you would be so transformed by the beauty and wonder of this world of spirit. You would experience your own brilliance and beauty."
5/29/2005

That hasn't happened as of this writing, but I wouldn't be surprised if it happened at any time.

The spirit world is a world that is more like the mind than the body. It's a place where thought and feeling play a more prominent role in life than here on the physical plane where so much of our daily lives are caught up in activities necessary to sustain our physical existence.

It is my understanding that spirits don't need to eat or sleep to maintain their lives, although they will do these things under certain circumstances. Spirits who cross over under traumatic conditions, or after a long illness, might spend a great deal of their early days sleeping, or peacefully resting, as Joshua did when he first arrived. So sleep is possible and available, but not necessary.

I have read of certain fruits available in the spirit world; when eaten they produce an emotional fulfillment in addition to being exceedingly delicious to taste. There are animals, trees, and flowers in abundance, but no rotting or decay.

There are beautiful homes, and some spirits enjoy living in homes that are copied from the homes they occupied during their earth life. If one desires to have a floral arrangement on a table, the flowers will last until the occupant sort of loses interest in that particular bouquet. Then the energy that composes these flowers will dissipate; the flowers disappear, but there is no slow decay or rotting, and no waste to dispose of.

If a community decides they want to construct a public building, spirits who might have been architects, designers, and artists will gather together at that site and project a mental form of the building they desire. Energy will then converge at that site, and form all the structures and details that the mental "blueprint" requires.

Spirits often work together in groups to accomplish tasks by pooling their energies. We have the example of the Council of Light that worked to facilitate the communication between Joshua and me through the "Letters." Joshua is now part of a "Task Force" that tries to prevent suicides from taking place. Dr. Carl Wickland had a group of spirits working with him called The Mercy Band that helped earthbound spirits ascend into the spirit world. A former chief psychiatrist at the National Psychopathic Institute of Chicago, Dr. Wickland documented his work with spirits in a fascinating book called *Thirty Years among the Dead*.

For more detailed descriptions of life in the spirit world, see *Life in the World Unseen* by Anthony Borgia. It is the account of Monsignor Robert Benson, son of the Archbishop of Canterbury. He died in 1914 and sent this book through Mr. Borgia as a way of correcting the mistaken concepts he had taught about the spirit world during his career as an Anglican minister.

29 COUNSELOR

We still contact Josh from time to time; like typical parents, we like to hear what he's been up to and whom he's hanging out with.

Getting along without Josh was very difficult, especially in the beginning. Sometimes Connie or I would be driving around town and pass a house or some other location associated with Josh and the tears would well up uncontrollably. I kept expecting that one day he would just come waltzing through the door of our home like nothing happened, and resume life where he left off.

From my viewpoint, I think Connie suffered a lot more than I did. She had a hard time rising above her grief. She began to worry that her grief might be creating a spiritual heaviness that would drag Josh down, hindering his progress in the spirit world.

"I'm fine, Mom, don't worry about it," he told her from the spirit world, when she asked him about it through a medium. "If it helps you, continue to tell yourself that I'm just away at school, but know this, it's a really great school." As a teenager Josh had loved to play electric guitar. We were delighted one day when he told us that he was learning to play the violin in the spirit world.

Josh couldn't understand why Connie had such a hard time getting over his passing. He addressed a lot of his communication to her, comforting her, and promising her that he was around her a lot, helping her. Connie decided she would let herself mourn for one year, and that's basically what she did, but Josh would tease her to make her laugh when she carried on beyond that time period. Connie is an abstract artist, and she titled one of her paintings *Seven Hundred Thirty Days*, for the second anniversary of his death. She did another one called *The Fourth Summer*, along the same lines.

When she completed the last mournful painting, Josh sighed and told her, "This is the last time, Mom, okay?" She's doing very well now, and her art career is advancing steadily.

I'm particularly fond of one of the paintings she did in tribute to Josh. It's called

I Love Everybody, which were the last three words of his suicide note. It gives the impression of a spirit soaring high above the trees in its ascension. Josh mentioned to us that, after he lit the match, he was pulled out of his body and could look down from above the trees. He was actually out of his body as the flames engulfed him, so he felt no pain. This, of course, was a great comfort to us.

I had several dreams during the first few weeks after he crossed over that shared a common theme of reconciliation in progressive stages. In the early dreams, Josh would just drift into the dining room of the house like nothing had happened, but he wouldn't interact with anyone. Then the dreams would progress to ones in which we looked at each other but exchanged no words. In later dreams, words of greeting might be exchanged and might include a light touch or a hand on the shoulder. In the last dream in this series, Joshua came right up to me, hesitated a little, and then reached out his arms to me. We fell into a full embrace, and the effect this dream had on me is indescribable. After this healing embrace, this particular series of dreams ended.

In less than a year Josh had progressed to the point where he spent a lot of his time helping other teen suicides make the transition to their new life in the spirit world.

One of the things I find most interesting about his activities revolves around his work with other suicides and the healing power of music in the spirit world. This is an excerpt from a letter we received through Ms. Haversham on May 30, 2004:

...Here, I am totally involved with others. At first I was involved with groups of young people who passed to this world in the same manner as me. It was like looking at myself over and over, and listening to many of the thoughts and crumpled ideas I had going in my mind over and over through the lives of these young people. On many levels I could confront and forgive myself for what I did. I could also reconcile my pain and anger and rebellion. I cried a lot together with other young people, and we raised ourselves into realms of higher consciousness. We moved into spaces of freedom (from our thoughts, emotions and regrets). Once we could move into higher realms of light and freedom, we could choose what to do...

I have visited realms of learning and of music and the arts. You know how I love music. This is a remarkable space to visit and study in.

The music is of such fine quality that it lifts our spirits and brings us into total love. It expresses beauty, love, peace, and joy, all at the same time. And everyone just lights up with it, so we then can take the music to a higher level. This is how it goes; we get lighter and lighter until we are totally in harmony and love. I could live in this realm forever, but it has a purpose. That is to give nourishment to our souls so that we can impart these virtues to those who we reach out to when we return to our realm of work.

I have chosen to work with young people. This is where I feel comfortable. I work one-on-one with each person. It is not as a professional, but as one who has learned from experience. So I have in my charge two or three young people at a time... They have all passed in the very recent past (within weeks of earth time). They also chose to take their life. Margo is the youngest, only 13. I listen to them, give them energy and comfort. This doesn't affect me as it did when I just came here. I feel totally free of all that heaviness. And since I can visit the realm of music and the arts, I am able to give them this light. Here it is like receiving food and nourishment.

There are other writings regarding the nature of the spirit world from sources that contain similar descriptions of the invigorating and healing nature of the energy that accompanies music in the higher realms.

Here is an excerpt from the book *Life in the World Unseen*, which was written through the mediumship of Anthony Borgia:

"Music being such a vital element in the world of spirit, it is not surprising that a grand building should be devoted to the practice, teaching, and the fostering of every description of music. The next hall that our friend took us into was entirely devoted to this important subject."

Monsignor Benson explains through Mr. Borgia that musical performances produce not just sound, but color and beneficial energy as well:

"...Unlike the earth where music can only be heard, there we had both heard and seen it. And not only were we inspired by the sounds of the orchestral playing, but the beauty of the immense form it created had its spiritual influence upon all who beheld it, or came within its sphere. We could feel this although we were seated without the theater. The audience within were basking in its splendor and enjoying still greater benefit from the effulgence of its elevating rays."

30 LIFE GOES ON

If you ask me how I am doing as of this writing, I would say that I am totally relieved of the concern that I had for Joshua's welfare after he crossed over. I am not totally healed of the tremendous longing I have to see his face, to kiss his cheek, to put my arms around him. Even though I can talk to him through spirit communication, it's not the same as having him here physically.

Sometimes I would sense him around me, especially in the first few months after his passing. There would be times when his photograph would catch my attention, his face almost alive with that mischievous smile. I would instinctively look at it and say, "Joshua, you beautiful boy!" I'd grab the frame, pick it up, and kiss him on the cheek. He even used my kissing of his picture as a cue to identify himself through another medium friend of mine in Raleigh.

That particular phenomenon still happens, but not as often anymore. I think Josh has reached the point where he doesn't need that sort of interaction as much anymore, and I honestly don't think about him as much as I used to. Things are bearable now; I'm not sure what shape I'd be in if I hadn't been able to make contact with him on the other side.

Nevertheless, there are days when I have a tremendous yearning for him and shed a few tears of longing, but these times of grief are fewer and fewer as time passes, and much less painful when they do occur. There is some truth to the old saying, "Time heals all wounds."

My other three children are a tremendous comfort. They've never told me this, but I'm pretty sure they have become very thoughtful about the effect any misbehavior on their part might have on Connie and me, considering the emotional turmoil we have gone through. They are very considerate when it comes to communicating with us, letting us know where they are and when they'll be home. They seem to be sensitive to the typical concerns we have as parents for their safety and well being. For this we are deeply grateful.

31 MEMO FROM JOSHUA

Joshua is now part of a "Task Force" of spirits who are focused on the issues of mental states in general and suicide in particular. On July 15, 2009, he spoke through an exceedingly gifted Raleigh, North Carolina medium, Cherie Lassiter, and he would like for me to paraphrase his comments here.

He says that it was a struggle and a fight for him to be on the planet. He saw our modern world as terribly competitive. It didn't sit well with him; having to be assertive to deal with all the competitive energy in society was not his way. He was a peaceful artistic soul, so the ambitious competitiveness didn't resonate with his spirit.

There was a physiological component in his brain as well that also a factored into his struggle. He describes it as a "brain formation" problem. His condition caused information to be perceived in a distorted way, so that he could not process it effectively. Because of this "brain chemistry" problem, his view of life emphasized the negative. Emotions like fear, anger, and frustration were close to the surface.

Being on the spirit side of things now, he can see that when he was alive, he wasn't seeing the whole picture of life. He was missing a great deal of the positive aspects of life – joy, laughter, love, optimism – and focusing on the negative.

The project he is working on now is not just to counsel suicides on the other side, but more importantly, to prevent suicides from taking place on the earth plane.

He wants to help young people in particular broaden their perceptions from only seeing the negative in life to recognizing the positive aspects as well. It is not inevitable that people will fall into these fear-based depressions. Focus on the good in life. Even those in depression can manage this state and find ways to rise above it.

He says that worse than depression is apathy. Young people can become apathetic and complacent, becoming numb and unfeeling. This dangerous state can lead to suicide.

"Don't absorb the negative crap in the culture," he says. You can choose to open your soul, and find ways to absorb joy and happiness instead. There is a tremendous amount of good and kindness in our modern world. It can be found with a little effort.

A most important tool in the pursuit of happiness is to find a place that involves coming out of ourselves and engaging others. When we concern ourselves with the needs of others, the grip of depression can no longer bind us down. As I mentioned in an earlier chapter, the simple act of making someone a cup of tea can rescue us from oblivion.

If we can find a place where we can employ our talents in the service of others, we will find ourselves on the path to inner peace and happiness.

32 WANTED: PIONEERS

When I began studying the subject of life after death, or what researchers refer to as survivability, over 30 years ago, it was a subject that was somewhat taboo. If you brought it up in conversation, you were given strange looks and lots of eye rolling. In recent years, the subject has become mainstream in the popular culture. It seems that movies and television shows are now full of content dealing with the spirit world. There is even a popular TV show called *Medium*, based on the work of a real-life psychic detective named Allison Dubois.

Spirit communication is still looked upon with skepticism in some scientific circles, partly because it is difficult to recreate the phenomena in laboratory settings. Nevertheless, the number of people who now accept the existence of the spiritual world, and our potential to communicate with it, is probably higher now than at any other time in modern history.

It is my hope that more and more people will feel called to do research in this field, to solve some of the many mysteries surrounding it. When people have direct experiences that convince them that life after death is a reality, they are often dramatic life-changing experiences, and the changes are for the better. As we discover that the priorities of those who inhabit the higher realms of the spirit world revolve around loving and serving others, we tend to embrace those priorities in our earthly lives as well.

I also look forward to progress in the field of Instrumental Transcommunication (ITC). There is a big difference between employing the talents of a medium and picking up a telephone and talking directly to someone in the spirit world, as has been experienced by some people in recent years. The great inventor Thomas Edison was working on a device for spirit communication, but died before he could complete it.

While I recommend mediums to people when I feel it would be beneficial to them, I don't advise taking every word as gospel truth.

When a spirit communicates through a medium, the content has to be translated according to the cultural background and life experience of that particular medium, and factual mistakes are common. In my view, the most important service a medium provides is the proof of survivability: Life after death–and in comforting family members and others when they discover that their loved one is still "alive" and in a good place.

EPILOGUE

33 PILGRIMAGE

If you take the Green Line from Blackfriars Bridge station heading westbound, the last stop on the London Underground is Wimbledon, the place of tennis fame. On Easter Sunday 2008, I made a pilgrimage there, but it had nothing to do with tennis.

Exiting Wimbledon station on a cold March morning, I crossed the street and headed to my left. Dodging traffic and walking past the upscale shops, I turned a corner and found what I thought to be Hartfield Road, although the lack of a signpost kept me guessing for many steps, until I found one further down the street. The row houses here appear to have been built in the 1930s, made of brick and crowned with the terra cotta-topped chimneys you find all over greater London.

About a fifth of a mile down the street on the right-hand side, there is a break in the seemingly endless wall of attached houses, and there stands a lone, small apartment building of perhaps four flats. Its plain, boxy architecture stands out in sharp contrast to the older houses on either side of it. The reason for the gap is sobering. This is where one of the thousands of bombs dropped on London by German planes fell during World War II, destroying the homes that once stood here. The apartments were built after the war in the space created by the bomb. The destination of my quest was not the apartment building, however.

Directly across the street on the left side of the road stands a small humble church wedged in between the row houses. Also built in the 1930s, this church at 136 Hartfield Road was partially destroyed during the Blitz, probably in the same raid that destroyed the houses across the street. Like innumerable places in London it has been rebuilt and enlarged, to continue its unorthodox mission.

For, you see, this is no typical church. This is the home of the Wimbledon Spiritualist Church, a church that practices mediumship as a central part of its ministry.

Opening the door, I entered into a large foyer inhabited by a handful of people waiting for the service to start.

A young woman named Karen approached and greeted me.

"The service will be starting in about 10 minutes," she said. "You can go on through the doors to the sanctuary if you like, or you're welcome to just wait here."

"I came all the way from the United States to attend your church," I said. "I've always wanted to visit a Spiritualist church, but there are none where I live."

"Really, how long are you in England for?" she asked.

"I'm here for just a few days with my wife. She's meeting some friends in the city right now. The trip is my gift to her for our 25th wedding anniversary. We're heading back home on Wednesday."

"How wonderful! Please make yourself at home," Karen said.

The walls of the foyer were covered with photographs. Some were large portraits of the church founder and other dignitaries. Others were simple snapshots of small groups of people posing together, the kind of photos you would expect from a wedding reception or even on the walls of a pub–people smiling and enjoying each other's company. I wandered over to a counter where I looked over some newsletters and other information pertaining to Spiritualism.

Seeing the young hostess was free, I walked over to talk to her some more.

"Karen," I asked, "how long have you been coming here?"

"About seven years, I think."

"What was it that brought you here?"

"Well, it was just after my mum died. I was having a rough go of it, and a friend told me about this place. When I attended the service, I was the first person the minister spoke to during clairvoyance. It was amazing! I've been coming here ever since."

"That's great," I said, "and I think you're doing a good job helping out here now."

I decided to go on into the sanctuary, and as I did so, I noticed a beautiful stained glass window of Jesus enshrined high upon the back wall. The light coming through the glass added a mystical quality to the scene. I took a seat in the third row and waited for the service to begin.

The congregation was small – less than 20 people.

The service was not unlike what you would find in a typical Protestant church–hymns accompanied by organ and piano, prayers, and a sermon. It was what happened after the sermon that was different.

"Now we will have clairvoyance," announced Karen, who was serving as master of ceremonies, from a podium on the right side of the altar area.

On the left, behind the main podium, sat a white-haired man wearing a clerical collar. He prayed or meditated for a couple of minutes, and then stood looking out over the congregation. Scanning back and forth across the pews a few times, his gaze finally settled on a man and woman sitting a couple of rows behind me.

"I'd like to address the couple sitting over here," he said, gesturing toward the couple. "Is that all right?"

"Yes," came the reply.

He concentrated for a few moments before speaking.

"I have here a gentleman." Then he paused again. Touching his chest, he spoke with confidence.

"I'm getting a feeling of tightness here," he said, "indicating this is someone who had a heart attack or maybe some lung problem like emphysema. Does that make sense to you?"

"Yes," said the man.

"He just wants you to know he's doing well now. The pain is completely gone, and you needn't worry about him anymore."

The minister moved on to a young man sitting behind me to my left, offering words of reassurance and encouragement.

"It's as if you've been going through a very difficult time recently. They want you to know that this period has now passed, and you are moving into a brighter phase of your life. Things are going to get much better now."

The young man appeared to be comforted by these words.

One by one, the minister went around the congregation. I'd say about half the group received a message from him, including me.

"They want you to know that for the last few months it's as if you've been a little withdrawn, kind of holding back," he said to me. "Now they're saying things are opening up for you. As if they're saying, 'Go for it!'"

This short message had a strong effect on me, and I noticed that I actually began acting with more confidence afterwards. In particular,

I returned to the process of writing this book with a clearer mind, and a renewed determination to finish it quickly.

After the service, we retired to the foyer for tea and biscuits. I pulled up my chair to a table where the president of the church was sitting with his wife and a couple of other parishioners. He was a large, good-natured man who in recent years had begun holding the mantle of leadership held by his father before him.

"I was elected, it wasn't an inheritance," he told me smiling. "How did you find us this morning?"

"I went on the internet. I was surprised to see that there must have been 15 Spiritualist churches in greater London alone."

"It's interesting," he said. "Spiritualism began in the United States in the 1840s with the Fox sisters, not in England. It spread to England from America. There are still many Spiritualist churches in America; I've visited several of them, although I must admit they can be hard to find sometimes."

"Yet it seems it has caught on more strongly here than in the U.S., doesn't it?" I asked and took a sip of my tea.

"Yes, that's true. I don't know why that is," he wondered aloud.

"I can see how Spiritualism can play an invaluable role in helping people heal from the pain caused by the loss of a loved one," I said.

"Well yes, exactly," he replied. "We're simply trying to help our fellow man recognize that there is survival–that is, that life goes on after physical death. That realization in itself is a great comfort to many people."

We talked a while longer, and the atmosphere felt as if I was among members of my own family, not strangers.

As I rose to depart I mentioned again how happy I was to finally experience a Spiritualist church.

"There are no Spiritualist churches that I know of in the Raleigh area," I said, "and yet, I am amazed at the number of people I run into in my community who are interested in things of a spiritual nature."

Then one of the ladies remarked, "You know, Ron, maybe you ought to put an ad in your local paper for all these people and just start one."

"You know, that's not a bad idea," I said, zipping up my jacket. "Who knows, maybe someday I will."

As I left the church and stepped into the cold London air, I could see my breath in front of me, and it felt as if it was going to snow.

I thought about what a coincidence it was that it was Easter Sunday, and that it had come so early this year. What was Easter if not the very day that Jesus demonstrated survivability, by appearing to his followers in spirit after his physical death?

Easter is associated with springtime and new life, with flowers and brightly colored eggs for the children. Yes, it was Easter. That seemed so appropriate, because after all that had happened since Joshua's passing, I felt like I was the one who had finally risen from the dead.

BIBLIOGRAPHY:

Borgia, Anthony, *Life In the World Unseen*, Midway, Utah, M.A.P., Inc., 1993.

Hose, David, *Every Day God*, Hillsboro, Oregon, Beyond Words Publishing, 2000.

Kubler-Ross, Elisabeth, *On Life After Death*, Celestial Arts, Berkeley, CA 1991.

Macy, Mark H., *Miracles in the Storm*, New York, New American Library, 2001.

Moody, Raymond A., Jr., M.D., *Life After Life*, New York, Bantam Books, 1975.

Spraggett, Allen, *The Bishop Pike Story*, New York, Signet, 1970.

Wickland, Carl A., M.D., *Thirty Years Among the Dead*, Amherst Press, 1924.

OTHER RECOMMENDED READING:

Brinkley, Dannion, *Saved by The Light*, New York, Harper Collins, 1994.

Egidio, Gene, *Whose Hands are These*, New York, Warner Books, 1997.

Ford, Arthur, *Unknown But Known*, New York, Harper and Row, 1968.

Morse, Melvin, M.D. *Where God Lives*, New York, Harper Collins, 2000.

Morse, Melvin, M.D. *Closer to the Light*, New York, Ivy Books, 1990.

FILMOGRAPHY:

Ghost (1990)

Sixth Sense (1999)

White Noise (2005)

ALSO RECOMMENDED:

What Dreams May Come (1998)

To reach Ron Pappalardo for speaking engagements,
telephone sessions, seminars, book signings, or to purchase
books, go to www.reconciledbythelight.com